P9-DML-857

[DOUBLE DETECTIVES]

The Danger on Shadow Mountain

by Zack Norris

STERLING CHILDREN'S BOOKS

New York

For Bill Luckey, my first Double Detectives editor, who gave the extended Carson family carte blanche to travel anywhere in the world ... and beyond!

STERLING CHILDREN'S BOOKS
New York

An Imprint of Sterling Publishing
387 Park Avenue South
New York, NY 10016

STERLING CHILDREN'S BOOKS and the distinctive Sterling
Children's Books logo are trademarks of Sterling Publishing Co., Inc.

© 2012 by Dona Smith

All rights reserved. No part of this publication may be reproduced,
stored in a retrieval system, or transmitted, in any form or by any means,
electronic, mechanical, photocopying, recording, or otherwise,
without prior written permission from the publisher.

ISBN 978-1-4027-9146-8

Distributed in Canada by Sterling Publishing
^{c}/$_o$ Canadian Manda Group, 165 Dufferin Street
Toronto, Ontario, Canada M6K 3H6
Distributed in the United Kingdom by GMC Distribution Services
Castle Place, 166 High Street, Lewes, East Sussex, England BN7 1XU
Distributed in Australia by Capricorn Link (Australia) Pty. Ltd.
P.O. Box 704, Windsor, NSW 2756, Australia

Ping-Pong® is a federally registered trademark first developed
by Parker Brothers, Inc. and now owned by Escalade Sports.

For information about custom editions, special sales, and premium
and corporate purchases, please contact Sterling Special Sales
at 800-805-5489 or specialsales@sterlingpublishing.com.

Designed by Susan Gerber

Manufactured in the United States of America

Lot #:
2 4 6 8 10 9 7 5 3 1
08/12

www.sterlingpublishing.com/kids

[Chapter One]

"It isn't whether you win or lose, but how you play the game." The speaker stared into the mirror over the mantel, lips twisted into a mocking sneer. "That's the most ridiculous thing I've ever heard. Anyone who believes that is nothing but a loser. The truth is just the opposite. In the end it doesn't matter a bit how you played the game, but whether you won or not. Winning is *everything*."

The mantel was crowded with trophies, but not many were for first place. "The losers lose because they haven't got the guts to go the distance. They're afraid to do *whatever* it takes to win, and that's why they will always be losers. That's why they go around saying 'blah-blah-blah, winning doesn't matter.' If they don't know they're lying then they deserve just what they get—*nothing*."

Reflected in the mirror was a face full of

self-satisfaction . . . and madness. "I'll beat anyone, and I'll get rid of anybody who tries to stand in my way. They won't even suspect that I'm up to something! I'm too smart for them. That's why I'm a winner. A winner never quits. A quitter never wins. No more second place for me!"

When the second-place trophy for the Wild-wood Snowboarding Competition was thrown across the room, it smashed through the glass coffee table. The neighbors jumped when they heard the sound of breaking glass and the wild, angry raving that came afterward. But they were used to hearing such noises from next door. They never complained. They were afraid to.

[Chapter Two]

Crystal clouds of snow plumed into the air as the three snowboarders sped down the mountain. They were crouched over their boards, knees bent, each one trying to remember to stay loose. They were racing on the black diamond run, the steepest run on the mountain, only for expert snowboarders. The three were experts, all right, fearless and highly skilled.

Swoosh! Otis raced out in front of his twin brother, Cody, while their cousin Rae trailed just behind. Cody was moving his body too much, and it was slowing him down. Rae was gaining on him fast, sticking out her arms for balance.

Otis pivoted on the top edges of the bumpy moguls to scrub up speed. He didn't want to look uncool by flailing his arms. He did look pretty uncool, though, when he lost control of his board and tumbled into the snow.

Rae and Cody shot past him. Otis picked himself up, dusted himself off, and looked after them. They were neck and neck. The two were waiting for him at the end of the run.

"I'm crazy about snowboarding," Otis said as he walked toward them. "I've fallen *head over heels* for it."

"You fell head over heels, all right." Rae smirked.

"Very *punny*," Cody replied. "Next time, instead of snowboarding down the mountain you should *sit on a potato pan, Otis.*"

"Sit on a potato pan, Otis" was Cody's favorite palindrome. He used it to tease his brother all the time. Cody loved making up palindromes—words or phrases that read the same backward and forward. His brother loved making up puns.

"C'mon, guys, let's head back to the lodge and warm up," Rae said.

The three trudged through the snow to the Shadow Mountain Resort, a large brick building with smoke coming out of the chimney. In the locker rooms they all stripped off their snow gear. Soon they joined the twins' father, Hayden Carson, and family friend Maxim Chatterton by one of the fireplaces in the lodge's large but cozy lobby.

Other guests wandered in and sat on couches or

at tables near the two other fireplaces, or next to the panoramic windows that looked out on the snowy landscape. Paintings of skiers and snowboarders decorated the walls. Mr. Carson had painted many of them.

Mr. Carson leaned back against the sofa. "You were out for a long time," he said to his twin boys and his niece, Rae Lee. "Glad to see you all looking so happy. I hope you can *stay* happy without finding any thieves, smugglers, forgers, or other crooks on this trip. I know that would make *me* happy."

Rae and the twins seemed to have a talent for getting mixed up in mysteries loaded with danger wherever they traveled. The three had tangled with kidnapping crooks on a Caribbean island, saving a movie star from harm. In the Amazon rain forest they had busted a ring of international animal smugglers. This time, Mr. Carson was hoping for a nice, quiet vacation.

"Try to confine your adventures here in Colorado to snowboarding and looking at nature," he said.

His son Cody wasn't paying attention. He was staring at the person who had just walked into the lobby of the ski lodge.

"It's Trent Margolis, the snowboarding champ," Cody said with awe in his voice. "That must be his coach with him."

Walking alongside Trent was a blond man with piercing dark eyes. His hands looked too big for him.

"I'm Cody Carson!" The twelve-year-old freckle-faced boy trotted toward them eagerly. "You're Trent Margolis! And you must be Coach Kent. It's so cool that your names rhyme—Trent and Kent. Easy to remember!"

Otis shook his head. "Aw, just look at him, Rae. He's acting like a little kid. The guy he's talking to could be the next Olympic snowboarding champion! This is embarrassing."

"You're Trent Margolis!" Cody repeated.

"Yeah, I know," drawled the snowboarder, tossing his curly black hair out of his eyes. He was wearing a gray hoodie and gray cargo-style vented pants that flared over his shred boots. Trent was sixteen and *very* full of himself.

Cody stepped back. He looked as if Trent had just smacked him in the face.

Trent's coach hurried past. "C'mon, Trent. We've got to go over today's training, so chop-chop." He nodded at Cody briefly without smiling as he and Trent walked away.

Cody's bruised enthusiasm was amped up by the sight of the other sixteen-year-old athlete who showed up next. "You're Joshua Crane!" he blurted, pointing a finger. "I'm Cody Carson, and I've been reading all about you. You're going to the Olympics!"

Otis groaned. How could his brother embarrass them all in front of two Olympic hopefuls? He glanced at his cousin Rae. She was looking at the ceiling.

The sandy-haired snowboarder was just a little bit shorter and more muscular than Trent. His hair was neatly trimmed, as though he had just gotten a haircut. He was wearing a black hoodie, and pants like Trent's in dark brown. He kept walking, eyes straight ahead, as if he hadn't heard anything.

"Hey, earth to Josh," said the bald man walking next to him.

Joshua paused. "Pardon me, Coach Renner. I was just thinking about how to improve my ten-eighty."

"Good idea. It needs improving," said the coach gruffly. He nodded in Cody's direction. "Say hello to your fan here."

Joshua looked at Cody as if seeing him for the first time. "Oh, hello, young man," he said quickly before walking away. Cody thought Joshua talked like someone his father's age. *Oh, hello, young man?*

Cody stared after him for a moment, and then whirled to look at the coach. "Wow, you were in the Olympics, like, before I was born, right?"

Otis groaned again. Was Cody going to be a dweeb

to everyone who had ever been or might one day be on the U.S. Olympic Team?

The coach laughed. "I was on the first Olympic snowboarding team, in 1998, so I guess it was before you were born," he said. He glanced at Cody's father and blinked. "Well, if it isn't Hayden Carson."

Mr. Carson nodded in surprise.

"I love your work," said the coach, extending his hand for a shake. "I saw some of your paintings at the Kenton-Ross Gallery in New York last year."

"Thank you," Mr. Carson said, shaking the man's hand. "I'm surprised that an Olympic coach has time to go to art galleries."

Coach Renner laughed. "Just one. My brother took me to your show when I visited him last year. Your photo and bio were there, and I have a good memory for faces. My brother is quite a fan of yours, and now I am, too."

"Well, thank you again." He nodded toward the twins. "My exuberant son is Cody, and this is his twin brother, Otis, and my niece, Rae. My sister's daughter often travels with us. And this is my agent and friend, Maxim Chatterton."

"Agent, friend, and all-around family helper," said the tall, gray-haired gentleman.

"Is this your first trip to the resort?" asked the coach.

"I often came to Shadow Mountain to ski, years ago," Maxim answered. "The owner, Oscar Fredrickson, became a friend. He told me that the young Olympic hopefuls would be here. I knew it would be a great surprise for the kids."

"I heard you'd be coming." The coach smiled. "I'm almost as excited about meeting Mr. Carson as Cody is about meeting Josh and Trent. We came here to train for the Silver Creek Challenge next month in Aspen. It gives us a chance to train our top contenders privately and give them more experience away from our home facility. Besides, it's kind of early in the season so it's pretty quiet here."

Maxim nodded. "I know you'll be practicing, but these three were hoping to get in plenty of snowboarding, too. Oscar said maybe they could go with your boys—when they are free, of course."

"Well, they'll be on the beginner's trail, or the intermediate, right?"

Otis spoke up. "No, we've been doing advanced runs for a year now," he said.

Coach Renner raised his eyebrows. "Well, Coach Kent and I were supposed to have exclusive access to the advanced area to train Josh and Trent." He rubbed his chin. "But I think we could work something out."

Cody's jaw dropped. "Wow!" He looked at his brother. "We're going to be with Josh and Trent!"

Don't jump up and down, Cody . . . please, Otis said to himself. "Thanks, Coach Renner. That's really great."

"Okay, see you later then," the coach said as he walked away. "Maybe you can give them a little competition," he said over his shoulder.

Otis looked at his brother and his cousin. "Did I hear him chuckle after he said that? If he did we'll have the last laugh. Maybe we're not training for the Olympics, but we're pretty good."

Cody shrugged. "I'm hungry. What's for dinner? *Go hang a salami. I'm a lasagna hog.*" He chuckled at his own goofy palindrome. He imagined himself snowboarding with the two Olympic hopefuls. *This is going to be a great vacation*, he thought. He didn't need any mysteries on this trip.

[Chapter Three]

"Hello! Hello!" A wiry gray-haired man with a mustache came rushing over. A wide smile stretched across his face. "Maxim Chatterton, my old friend," he cried as he patted Maxim's shoulder. "It's been too long!"

"Hello, Oscar, it certainly has been a long time. I've missed the place. This is Hayden Carson, his twin boys, Cody and Otis, and his niece, Rae Lee. They're looking forward to doing some snowboarding with those young champions."

The owner, Oscar Fredrickson, welcomed everyone to the Shadow Mountain Resort. "I'm sorry I wasn't here when you arrived yesterday. I hope you have plans to do some painting, Mr. Carson."

"I'll certainly make some sketches. The mountain scenery is marvelous. So is your lodge."

"Thank you. Shadow Mountain is the oldest resort in the area, built in 1919. It's very small and very exclusive."

"It's also *very* cool," said Otis. He looked up at the high arched ceiling with a stained-glass skylight, and then gazed out one of the huge picture windows.

The sun was setting on the mountain, painting the sky with plumes of pink and gold. The snowy peaks shimmered as though dusted with diamonds.

"Tell us about the terrain park," Cody said.

"We ride at the advanced level. We've been snow-boarding since we were little kids," Otis explained.

"Oh . . . I'm so sorry"—the man tugged at his mustache—"but I promised Coach Renner and . . ."

"We just met Coach Renner," Cody interrupted. "He told us he'd work something out so we could use the park with Josh and Trent."

"Well, that's very kind of him." Oscar rubbed his hands together and smiled again. "I've just had the advanced-level terrain park completely redone. It's called Halo, and you get there by taking lift number two. You're going to love it," he said, smiling broadly.

"Let me give you a rundown of the features: You start out with a forty-foot jump and end with a thirty-foot jump. In between you've got a couple of back-to-back kickers, forty-foot and forty-five foot. Then there's a sixteen-foot mailbox, a twenty-foot c-box, a twenty-four-foot battleship rail, and a sixteen-foot wall. What do you think of that?"

"Awesome!" said Cody.

"Maxim said you have a half-pipe, too," Otis said.

"Oh, yes. It's pretty spectacular—a four-hundred-foot half-pipe with twelve-foot walls."

"We can practice our spins and grabs, and the somersault we learned," Otis said.

"You can start tomorrow morning," said Oscar, twirling the end of his mustache. "By the way, we have a game room with a Ping-Pong table and a pool table. It's always stocked with video games—but our satellite TV is conked out, and I'm afraid we need a new one."

"No big deal. We love video games almost as much as we love snowboarding," Rae told him. She smoothed her short dark hair.

"What a talented bunch you are!" Oscar patted her shoulder. "Dinner service starts in an hour. I'll put you near the table where Trent and Joshua eat with their coaches. Their families eat at a separate table so the boys can go over the day's training at dinner."

"Seems strange that they wouldn't eat with their families." Mr. Carson took a step back.

Oscar sighed. He glanced around, then stepped closer to the group and spoke softly. "It's all about training, training, training with those boys." He waved a hand in the air. "In my opinion they are much too serious. I know they want to win and go to the next

Olympics, but snowboarding should be fun, too. I think those boys are under too much pressure. It could make them sick. The way they get yelled at and criticized—well, you'll see. I'll talk to you later."

Oscar was hurrying toward the dining room but stopped suddenly and spun around. "Wait! I forgot to tell you something important! Your cell phones won't work here. The people in the area do not like the look of cell phone towers on the mountain. I think it's crazy, but I can't talk them into it. Fortunately, people come here in spite of the inconvenience."

"It's just like the old days when I used to come here. There were no cell phones at all then," said Maxim.

Cody, Otis, and Rae exchanged glances. They found it hard to imagine a world without cell phones.

"Yes, it's just like the old days." Oscar nodded. "Another thing just like the old days is that there are cougars nearby. You won't run into them unless you travel beyond the freeride area beside the half-pipe. There are avalanches in the area, too. There are plenty of signs telling you where not to go, and the area is blocked off with yellow tape. Every once in a while somebody decides to venture into the forbidden area. Don't let it be you."

"I read about avalanches before the trip," Rae piped up. "I found out some interesting stuff."

"You did?" Cody raised his eyebrows.

"You never mentioned reading about avalanches," Otis said. He wasn't all that surprised. Rae would read the list of ingredients on a box of laundry detergent if she couldn't get her hands on anything else. She was a fountain of trivia and random knowledge.

"The biggest avalanche was in 1980, in Washington State," said Rae. "It was set off by the eruption of Mount Saint Helens. In some places it left snow six hundred feet deep." She paused to gauge the reaction from the others. All were staring at her, not moving a muscle. "I've read about other avalanches in the 1960s and 1970s that some rescuers claim were even bigger."

"I think that's enough about avalanches," said Maxim. "Let's head back to our rooms and get ready for dinner."

"I'll see you all later." Oscar beamed at them.

Maxim, Mr. Carson, and Rae each had their own rooms. Cody and Otis shared one.

"This room is so great," Otis said as soon as they stepped into 214. The room was huge, with twin beds and woven throw rugs. There were beams overhead and arched windows with a view of the mountain. A doorway led to the porch.

"The tub is as big as a swimming pool!" called Cody from the bathroom.

"It's big, all right, but not *that* big," Otis said. He plopped down on one of the beds, and Cody threw himself down on the other.

"You acted like a little kid in a toy store when you met Joshua and Trent," Otis said, frowning. " 'You're Trent Margolis! You're Joshua Crane!' " he mimicked, clapping his hands and squealing.

Cody lay back lazily. "Oooh, like you're just too grown up to get excited about meeting two guys who are probably going to be in the next Olympics. And they are only a few years older than we are! Get over yourself." He looked up at the ceiling. "I love Deerville, but it's great to be here. If everybody at DD could see me talking to Trent Margolis and Joshua Crane . . ."

Cody imagined his classmates at the Deerville Day School—in upstate New York, working on their assignments and taking tests at that very moment. He was grateful that the private school, famous for its musicians, writers, and painters, allowed him, his brother, and cousin to travel with their dad as long as their homework was done and e-mailed in on time.

"I think those guys are the ones who need to get over themselves," said Otis. "That Trent guy acted like he was just too cool, and Joshua—he talked like somebody Dad's age. 'Oh, hello, *young man.*' "

He paused for a moment and then added, "All that pressure must be tough on them, though. I wouldn't like to get yelled at all the time."

Cody started putting shirts into a drawer. "Yeah, well, I wouldn't mind if I had the chance to be in the Olympics," he said.

Otis jumped up and unzipped his bag. "I bet you would after a while." He opened the closet door and then suddenly stood still. "Hey, listen," he whispered. "People are arguing in the hall."

The two boys were very quiet. The voices got louder and louder. One of them was Joshua's.

"I'm getting tired of it day after day after day. The man acts like he's already my father."

Cody and Otis looked at each other and frowned.

"What man is he talking about?" Cody whispered.

"Shhh!" hissed Otis.

"Well, he's going to be your father when we get married, Joshua. Frank is just trying to be helpful. He just doesn't want the coach to be too hard on you."

"Who's Frank?" asked Cody.

Otis shushed him. "I guess Joshua's mother is talking about her fiancé."

"That's right! He *doesn't* understand," said Joshua. "It's bad enough with Coach Renner on my back every minute. Then Frank is always riding him, telling him to take it easy, which only makes him mad. Frank keeps giving me pep talks, too. Like I need his input."

"Watch your tone, Joshua. I don't like expressions such as *riding him*. If you believe Frank is annoying the coach or criticizing him excessively, then say so. Don't talk about him *riding* the coach. You'll sound uneducated. People will judge you by the way you speak, so speak like a gentleman."

Cody and Otis exchanged glances. "So *that's* why he talks that way," Cody muttered.

Joshua raised his voice. "Trent says I talk like somebody's dad. Speaking of *dads*, tell Frank to quit borrowing my stuff—my gloves, my hat, my jacket. And tell him to stop butting in on my training. Just let the coach yell if he wants. I can take it."

"If you'd work harder, the coach wouldn't yell so much. This training is serious business, Joshua. You don't get to the Olympics by treating a sport as a hobby. Besides, Coach Renner isn't getting any younger. You may be his last hope of coaching an Olympic athlete."

"I'm *not* treating it like a hobby!" Joshua exploded. "I work as hard as Trent, and his coach yells at him, too."

"Well, I know it makes you nervous. You threw up after dinner a few days ago. Really, Joshua, you *do* need to toughen up. You can't get rattled so easily."

"Between you and Coach Renner and Frank,

someone is at me every minute. I know Frank is trying to be nice, but he just makes things worse. I want you all to leave me alone for a while!"

The twins heard the sound of running footsteps. "Come back here!" the woman called. Then the sound of swift, choppy footsteps passed the door.

"Whoa!" Cody said after a moment. "Joshua's mother sure pushes him."

"Yeah," Otis agreed. "She really wants him to be a winner."

Cody cracked open the door, and he and Otis peered into the hallway. They saw a short blond woman in very high heels bustling along. "How can she walk so fast in those stupid shoes?" asked Cody.

"Got me." Otis closed the door.

Cody took some clothes from his bag and opened another drawer. "I think Joshua should *thank* that Frank guy for trying to take the pressure off."

Otis tightened a shoelace. "Right, but I know what he means. He doesn't want the coach to think he's wimpy. And having an almost-but-not-quite stepdad along for the trip must be hard, too. Anyway, let's go down to the dining room. I'm ready for dinner."

"I'm ready for dessert," said Cody.

People were beginning to crowd into the dining room. Oscar was speaking sternly to a chubby guy with brown hair. He looked to be about eighteen years old.

"Carl, stay out of the kitchen. You shouldn't be eating between meals anyway."

Carl walked away angrily.

"That's Carl, one of the lift operators." Oscar sighed when he saw the boys. "He would eat all the time if we let him." Then his face brightened suddenly. "Oh, hello there, Ms. Margolis." The kitchen door swung closed behind a small, slender woman. Oscar tilted his head to one side. "Not that it matters, but what were you doing in the kitchen?"

"Oh, I was walking by and I remembered that I wanted to ask the head chef for the stuffed cabbage recipe. I just popped in for it—but he wasn't around."

"The head chef is off today, but I'll get the recipe for you later. By the way, Ms. Margolis, these are Hayden Carson's boys, Cody and Otis."

The woman shook hands with each of them. "I'm Trent's aunt. Call me Maggie." The family resemblance was easy to see. She had Trent's curly black hair.

Rae had just walked in, and Cody motioned her over. "Hey, Rae, this is Trent's aunt Maggie."

Mr. Carson and Maxim arrived, and Cody introduced them, too. "Since the boys eat dinner with their coaches," said Mr. Carson, "I hope that you'll have dinner with us."

"That would be nice, thank you," Maggie replied.

The six of them chose a table near the picture window that offered a view of the mountain. They noticed that Trent and his coach sat several tables away from Joshua and Coach Renner.

"I think it's strange that the boys don't eat dinner with relatives, but with the coaches instead," said Mr. Carson. "After all, they're with them all day. Shouldn't they get a little time off?"

Maggie shook her head. "The coaches know what they're doing," she said firmly. "If Trent wants to be a serious athlete, he has to be one hundred percent committed. They aren't here to have fun."

The waiter came to take their orders. When he was gone, Maggie went on talking.

"Besides, Joshua Crane is a teammate, but a competitor, too." She leaned forward. "I wouldn't be surprised if he and his coach resorted to a bit of trickery to get ahead."

"Goodness, what kind of trickery?" Maxim asked.

"Oh—I'm not sure," she said, tapping her fingers on the table. "Trent has had some bad luck since he's been here—skin rashes, stomach trouble."

"That could be nerves," said Otis, thinking of the conversation he'd overheard between Joshua and his mother. "The competition coming up is a bigger deal than anything they've been in before, isn't it?"

"Yes, but"—she folded and refolded her napkin— "it's just a feeling. I don't trust Joshua's pushy mom, either." She sat back in her chair. "There is a lot of money from sponsors to think about."

She looked over at the table where Trent sat with his coach. "Coach Kent does his best for Trent, though sometimes I wish he'd push him a little harder. He makes sure he only eats healthy meals, and even makes him a special vitamin drink. He is trying to help him get sponsors, too. The right companies can be very, very helpful with money."

Mr. Carson sipped from his glass of water. "What do you do for a living, Maggie?" he asked, changing the subject.

"I'm a writer," she said. "I've published several novels. In fact, they're best sellers." She blushed. "Writing allows me to travel with Trent to his competitions."

"Tell us what you've written!" Rae said eagerly.

"Let's not talk about my books now," she said. "We were talking about Trent, weren't we, Mr. Carson?"

"Yes. If you don't mind my asking, where are his parents?"

"It's not a happy story," Maggie began.

The waiter appeared and began serving the food.

"Chicken for the lady, roast beef for the gentlemen, burgers for everyone else."

"Thank you," said Mr. Carson. Then he turned to Maggie. "You were saying?"

Maggie took a deep breath. "Trent is an orphan. His parents died when he was quite young."

"Our mother died when we were young, too." Otis smoothed his napkin in his lap.

"I'm so sorry."

Otis shook ketchup onto his burger. "We were babies. We really don't remember her. Sometimes I think I've dreamed about her, though."

"Me, too," said Cody. He shifted in his seat. "What happened to Trent's parents?"

Maggie moved her water glass in a little circle. She was silent for so long that the others started to get uncomfortable.

"What happened, Maggie?" Mr. Carson prompted.

Maggie took a deep breath. "They were poisoned."

[Chapter Four]

"What?" Otis jumped in his chair.

"It was an accident," Maggie said quietly. "Trent's father, my brother Eric, was interested in edible wild plants." She sighed. "But he didn't know as much as he thought he did. One day Eric picked some mushrooms in the woods and . . . he and his wife died soon after eating them. The mushrooms were death cap."

Mr. Carson's mouth dropped open.

"Shocking, isn't it?" Maggie said. She shook her head slowly. "It was so senseless. Anyway, Trent was provided for. My brother and his wife were well off, and Trent has a trust fund. He can get along on that for now. When he turns eighteen he'll inherit quite a bit of money, too." She smiled. "He won't have to worry about sponsors to pay for expenses anymore."

"It's too bad about his parents," Rae said.

"Yes, it is," Maggie said. She leaned forward. "I'm

Trent's only living relative. He's like my own child. I want him to have everything he wants—and he wants to go to the Olympics. Winning this competition in Aspen is an important step."

A waiter walked over to Trent's table. "Coach Kent, you have a phone call. It's someone from Keller Sporting Goods," he announced rather loudly.

"I'll take it," the coach said. He stood up and nodded to Trent, then turned to walk away.

"Oh, Kent," called Coach Renner. "You know the Keller Sporting Goods Company has been talking to Joshua." His voice was level but his eyes smoldered.

The coach looked at Renner, a little half-smile on his face. Then he shrugged and turned away. A few minutes later he came striding into the dining room, beaming. "They're interested," he said, clapping Trent on the shoulder. "They still want to see how you do in Aspen, but I think it's a done deal. They're talking about a lot of cash." He whispered something in Trent's ear.

Trent's eyes widened. "Wow . . . that's awesome."

"Sounds like good news!" Maggie said to the group.

Moments later the words "You know, I don't feel well" came from Trent's table.

"Wha—" Maggie turned. Everyone in the dining room was looking at Trent. He was doubled over.

"Trent!" Maggie jumped up and rushed to his side.

"It must be nerves again," said Coach Kent. "We've got to get him to relax."

"Come on, try to get up," Maggie coaxed. "I'll take you upstairs. You'll be fine."

Trent groaned, but he got to his feet. Maggie slowly led him from the dining room. The tall athlete shuffled along, slumped over Maggie's small frame.

"She should take him to the doctor," Otis said. "Trent was drinking something from a glass bottle— green stuff," he observed. "Maybe it didn't agree with him. Or maybe it was . . ."

"Poisoned?" Rae rolled her eyes. "Would someone really do that?"

"I certainly hope not," said Maxim. "I think you're jumping to conclusions here, Otis."

Mr. Carson nodded. "Maybe Maggie got you going with all her talk about trickery and poisoning. She *was* a little morbid during our first meeting if you ask me."

Otis folded his napkin and put it beside his plate. "Both sides want a win in Aspen. It means sponsor money, too. Maybe someone is willing to go pretty far to get what they want."

"We saw that lift operator, Carl, come out of the kitchen right before dinner," mentioned Cody.

"And Maggie, too," Otis added.

"Why would a ski-lift operator poison Trent? He doesn't have anything to gain," said Rae. "And what about Maggie? Come on, she's his aunt."

Otis wouldn't give up. "I don't know about the lift operator," he said. "But he was in the kitchen so he *could* have put something in Trent's drink. I don't really think Maggie did anything, but look at it from a detective's point of view."

"Do tell," Rae said, crossing her arms.

Otis put his elbows on the table. "She has a motive. Think about it. If she is Trent's only living relative, that money he's going to inherit would be all hers."

"But Maggie said she's had several successful novels published," Maxim pointed out.

"That's what she *said*." Otis took another bite and chewed thoughtfully. "Of course, people lie all the time, especially villains. They don't come right out and tell you they're planning to commit a crime."

"True." Rae nodded.

Maxim sighed. "Can we please forget about poisoning Trent until *after* dinner?"

"All right," Otis said. He looked over to where Joshua's mother and her fiancé were sitting. "I notice that Joshua's mother keeps looking at her engagement ring and fiddling with it. We overheard her talking to Joshua about getting married to someone named

Frank. That must be him." He glanced over and saw the man hand the waiter his credit card.

Maxim sighed. "Yes, I ran into Mrs. Crane and her fiancé. His name is Frank Warren. He seems quite nice. However, I suspect that Mrs. Crane keeps looking at the engagement ring he gave her because she knows it isn't real."

"Did he *say* it was a diamond?" Mr. Carson asked.

"Apparently so," Maxim answered. "When we met he even suggested that I look at her magnificent diamond. Mrs. Crane didn't speak up, but I thought that I could sense in her face that she knew it was a fake."

"It's a strange lie to tell," said Mr. Carson.

"Yes," Maxim said. "However, it's likely not as bad as it seems at first. Mrs. Crane isn't a wealthy woman. Mr. Warren may not be wealthy either. Maybe he couldn't afford an expensive ring, but he wanted to impress her."

Cody knitted his brows. "How do you know all this about Mrs. Crane and Mr. Warren?"

"Ha!" Maxim leaned forward. "I was walking behind two of the maids. Maids know everything because people don't usually bother to hide anything from them. They overhear conversations, see people's medicines, even what's in their trash cans."

"You're right," said Mr. Carson. "I don't pay much attention to the maids."

Maxim nodded. "They overheard Mrs. Crane say she was hoping for sponsors to help with Joshua's expenses. They also heard her telling someone on the phone that she thought her diamond was a fake."

"Lying about *anything* is a bad sign," Otis said.

Mr. Carson agreed. Out of the corner of his eye he saw a figure coming toward them. "Hush, everyone," he said quietly. "Mr. Warren is heading our way."

Frank Warren was a man of average height. In fact, everything about him was average, from head to toe. He had brown hair cut short, wore a plain sweater and beige pants, and had pale gray eyes. He was the kind of man who would blend into any crowd.

When he neared the table he smiled, revealing a row of perfect white teeth. The smile lit up his face, somehow changing his appearance. Friendliness seemed to glow around him.

"Hi, I'm Frank Warren. I saw you all here with Hayden Carson and I just had to come over and introduce myself. Mr. Carson, your paintings are unbelievable. I go to every show I can."

"Thank you." Mr. Carson smiled back at him. He introduced Rae and the twins.

Otis studied the man's face. "You look kind of familiar."

Mr. Warren shrugged. "Well, I know a lot of people who look like me. But maybe you saw me at one of your dad's shows."

Otis shrugged. "Maybe," he said doubtfully.

"You're all going to have a great time," said Mr. Warren. "Coach Renner told me you'll be using the terrain park with Joshua and Trent."

"We can hardly wait," said Cody.

"Maybe we can all have lunch or dinner together sometime, Mr. Carson." He looked back to his table, where Mrs. Crane was still fiddling with her ring. "I don't want to leave my fiancée alone. It was nice to meet you all." He smiled again and walked away.

"Nice fellow," Mr. Carson remarked.

"Indeed," said Maxim. "What personality he has. He just lights up, doesn't he? Earlier, I heard him tell Joshua's coach to take it easy on him." Maxim sipped his glass of water. "It seems to me that he's the only one in the group who is being reasonable about this snowboarding training." He looked around the table. "What is everyone doing tomorrow?"

"I'm going to bundle up and get out there with my sketch pad," said Mr. Carson. "I'd love to draw some of the animals and birds around here, but I'll definitely be avoiding the cougars."

"Oh yes, do avoid the cougars," said Maxim. "I'm going to try some skiing."

Cody, Otis, and Rae talked about snowboarding. But Otis didn't say a word about a plan he'd been hatching. He figured if the three of them got out early and went over the course in the terrain park, it would show Joshua and Trent that they were serious snowboarders.

As they got up to leave, they caught sight of Coach Renner leaning back in his seat with his arms crossed over his chest. Joshua had left the table. The coach was staring at Coach Kent. He had a smile on his face but not in his eyes.

Coach Kent glared angrily at him, clenching and unclenching his fists. It looked like there would be a fight for sure. But there wasn't. Coach Kent just turned and stomped out of the dining room.

"Did you see the look on Coach Kent's face?" Rae whispered to the twins.

"Yeah, but what about Coach Renner?" Otis said. "He looked like he was pretty pleased with what went down." He looked off into space for a moment. "Anybody think Coach Renner poisoned Trent?"

"No," Cody said firmly. "He was an Olympic snowboarding champion."

"That doesn't mean he couldn't poison somebody," said Rae. "I don't think he did, though."

They all ran into Mr. Warren on the porch a few minutes later. Maxim told him what had happened between the two coaches. "I really feared they would come to blows," he said.

Mr. Warren waved a hand dismissively. "These coaches are nuts," he said. "I want both of the boys to do well in Aspen. I don't want them taking the competition too seriously, though. It leads to a bad attitude, bad sportsmanship, and even bad health. Last year Trent's coach worked him so hard before a competition that he pulled a muscle and had to sit it out. I try to get Coach Kent to take it easier on Trent, but he won't listen." He shook his head.

"Coach Kent was so angry, he left without paying the bill or tipping the waiter," said Maxim. He had been a waiter once when he was young, and he disapproved of anyone who didn't leave a tip.

Mr. Warren did a double take. "Yikes! I got so distracted with everything that was going on that *I* forgot to leave a tip, too. Let me get back there before everyone leaves." He hurried away.

"You see?" said Maxim. "The fellow doesn't want the boys to be pushed too hard to win. He's the only one who's sane."

"Uh-huh," Otis said quickly. "Cody, Rae, listen—I've got to check something out. I'll see you guys in the game room in a few minutes, okay?" He was on his way before they could answer.

✳

When they met in the game room, Otis told the others what he had found out. "I went on all of the book-seller sites that I know. I didn't find a single book by Maggie Margolis."

"Hmm . . ." Rae tucked a piece of her short dark hair behind her ear. "Maybe she uses a pen name. You know, another name she uses to write books."

Otis slapped his forehead with his hand. "Duh! I didn't think of that."

"Too busy playing detective?" Cody asked, chuckling. "We can ask Maggie about her pen name next time we see her."

"Yeah, I guess so," Otis replied. "Let's get to the park super early. We'll show the guys and their coaches what we can do."

[Chapter Five]

Early the following morning, Otis led the way to the ski lift. He, Cody, and Rae were all wearing fleece hoodies and fleece-lined pants over their long underwear. Goggles were tipped up over helmets, and all wore waterproof gloves.

"By the time they get to the park we'll already be on the course." Otis smiled. "Maybe we can't be as fancy with our tricks, but we're not too shabby."

The others nodded.

"Maybe that will get them over their attitudes," Rae said, adjusting her helmet.

"They had attitudes, I have to admit," Cody said, pulling up his gloves. "I don't know how they can see with their noses so far up in the air."

Otis snorted. "Oh, it didn't bother you yesterday. 'I'm Cody Carson, please say hello to me, Trent! Can you see me, Josh?'" he said in a singsong voice.

"Cut it out, I wasn't *that* bad," Cody said, pretending to examine his snowboard.

"Oh, yes you were, dude," Otis shot back.

"They didn't even say hello when we passed them on the way to the dining room this morning. They treated us like *losers*," Rae said.

"*I'm a dud, am I?*" Cody said, pleased to find a way to use a new palindrome he'd come up with. "That's what they think, but they're wrong. Well, we'll show them."

"Let's get to the top of the mountain," said Otis. "It's all *downhill from there*—especially for Cody."

"I think someone who *fell head over heels for snowboarding* should watch what he says," Cody shot back.

"Enough, you guys!" said Rae. She gave the twins a look that shut them both up. They reached the lift just as the operator arrived.

"Hi, I'm Carl," said the chubby guy. "I heard about you guys. You're here with some big-deal painter."

"He's our dad—my brother's and mine," said Cody. "Rae is our cousin."

Carl rocked back on his heels. "I'll bet staying in the same lodge with Tweedledumb and Tweedledumber isn't the big whoop you thought it would be. I'm talking about our two Olympic champs. Those guys are a pain. I'd like to . . . well, I don't want to get aggravated first thing in the morning. They'll be along soon enough."

"We're going to show them we can handle ourselves in the park," said Otis firmly.

Carl blinked. "Why don't you try the half-pipe first," he said. "They're pretty particular about getting over the jibs and jumps and all as soon as they're ready."

"We'll be done soon," said Rae. "It wouldn't kill them to wait a few minutes, anyway."

She released her rear foot from its binding and checked to make sure that the front binding was fastened tightly before sliding closer to the lift. The others did the same, pushing off with the right foot in the snow, left foot on the board.

"Really, you guys should start on the half-pipe," repeated Carl. "They're going to be very mad if they have to wait."

"They'll just have to deal," said Rae.

She, Cody, and Otis folded down the back part of the rear binding on their boards. They stepped behind the red line and looked over their shoulders, watching the chair approach. The operator gave the go-ahead, and they moved forward. When the chair hit the back of their knees, they sat down and lowered the safety bar in front of them. Each one raised the tip of the board so that it wouldn't catch in the snow.

Carl called after them as the lift began to move. "Say hi to Mike when you get off. He's the operator up the mountain."

"Those guys must have scared Carl," said Otis as he rested his right foot on his board's stomp pad. "He seems kind of afraid of them."

"He doesn't like them, that's for sure," said Cody.

They rode in silence for the rest of the trip up the mountain, mentally reviewing technique.

Soon it was time to get off the lift. They leaned forward a bit and allowed the chair to give them a push. Then they slid down the ramp and moved off to the side to put their rear feet back into the bindings.

"Carl wanted us to say hello," called Cody.

Mike, thinner and older than Carl, waved back. "You all know what you're doing?"

"We do," Otis answered. He moved to where the course started. The others followed. Otis glided toward the first rail, a twenty-foot straight. He ollied up on the rail, first shifting his weight to his back leg and picking up the nose of the board. When he was airborne he leveled the board and bent his knees up to his chest, landing flat on the rail.

He whirled into a one-eighty grind, riding backward along the length of the board and then spinning around to land facing forward. Keeping low and centered on his board, he sped along toward the forty-five-foot kicker. As he moved into the jump, he pushed forward from his back knee and launched into the air. Then he bent at the waist, tucked his chin to his chest, and somersaulted into a forward flip.

As soon as he landed, he got ready for the forty-foot kicker. This time, while soaring in the air he turned his shoulders and spun into a corkscrew.

I'm really in the zone, he thought proudly. He ollied onto the rail, popping the front end and landing flat. Then he slid along the rail and opened his shoulders forward, turning the back of the board perpendicular to the rail. When he neared the end of the board, he turned his shoulders sideways and ollied off.

I'm nailin' this, Otis thought. He hoped Trent and Joshua were watching. The battleship rail was coming up. This rail kinked up, then went flat, then kinked down, in a shape that looked a bit like a battleship. Otis rode straight over it and got ready for the wall.

Rock to fakie was his favorite wallride trick. It was lots of fun, and he could make it really styley. The wall was nearly straight up, at about a seventy-degree angle to the ground. He rode up to it, making sure not to go *too* fast. Once he got to the coping at the top edge, he leaned a bit forward up on his front binding and brought the tail of the board up. Then came back in fakie, rocking to the base of the wall, and rode away.

Up in front was the last jump, a thirty-footer. Otis prepared for his big finish. He was going to do a misty flip. It was a dazzling combination of flips and spins. He would fly through the air and land on the giant air bag. *Once those two guys see what the three of us can do on this terrain, they won't be so snippy*, he thought.

Suddenly, everything went wrong. Otis's board caught on something underneath the snow, and he went tumbling down the mountain. He kept his body loose, as he'd been taught to do, and fell forward. His body was bumping over hard lumps underneath the snow. He hit his chin, and his teeth clamped together, nicking the edge of his tongue. He tasted blood in his mouth. He heard a shriek behind him, and then a thud.

As he rolled to a stop, he saw that Cody had fallen, too. Instead of rolling, he was sliding headfirst down the mountain. His arms were stretched straight out in front of him. His snowboard was bouncing behind him.

Cody was still skidding when Rae dropped. Otis

could see her lean forward, but as her board hit something under the snow she jerked backward. Rae shouted as she fell on her seat, then her back hit the snow.

Otis scrambled to his feet. Cody slid to a stop beside him and rolled onto his back. Otis reached down to help him up, but Cody waved him off. All the wind had been knocked out of him.

Rae slid beside Otis and Cody. She groaned as she pushed herself into a sitting position. She was breathing hard. Rae lifted her goggles and looked at Otis. "What was *that?*" she gasped.

Cody sat up and slid his goggles onto his forehead. "My snowboard hit something under the snow and then, *blam*! I lost control and hit the ground." He stood up slowly. "I feel a little shaky."

"So do I," said Rae. "That was scary. I was cruising along and then, *bang*! I fell down. It all happened so fast." She held out a hand, and Otis grabbed it and helped her up.

"There were definitely hard lumps under the snow," she said. "They must have been rocks, and they sure didn't get there by accident."

[Chapter Six]

Otis, Cody, and Rae dusted the snow off their jackets and pants. "Anybody hurt?" Otis asked.

"Nope," said Rae. "I'm just a little shook up."

"So am I," said Cody. "But you're bleeding, Otis."

"I just bit my tongue. No big deal."

Josh, Trent, and their coaches were watching. The boys each wore a cocky half-smile. Rae and the Carsons didn't like it one bit.

"It seems like the three of you have trouble staying upright," Josh said. He opened his eyes wide. "It must be difficult to snowboard when you keep falling over. Maybe you should all go over to the beginner's area and get some practice.'"

"Um, it's snow*board*, not snow*butt*." Trent chuckled.

"I'm getting *board*, and I mean *bored* with their attitude, guys. I don't like being the *butt* of their jokes, either," Otis grumbled to Rae and Cody.

"Hey, pretty good puns," Trent said appreciatively. "Y'know, it's too bad you're not that clever on a board."

"Excuse me!" Rae put her hands on her hips. "You're both lucky it wasn't one of you falling over those rocks!"

"They've both got rocks in their heads," Otis muttered.

"Uh-oh, he's funny *again*," said Trent. "You *rock* at jokes—just not on a snowboard."

"See for yourself," said Cody, pointing. "There are rocks under the snow. That's why we all fell."

"Rocks?" Coach Renner marched over to where Cody was pointing. He got down on one knee and brushed the snow aside.

"Kent, come over and look at this." He eyed the other coach with a look of suspicion. "Have you got any idea how these got here? They must have been put here just before the snowfall last night. There are about two inches of flakes covering these rocks." Coach Renner took off his ski hat and ran a hand over his bald head.

Coach Kent shot him a look full of daggers. "I don't like what you're suggesting, old man," he snapped. He knelt down and took a look. "You're right. This stuff didn't land here on its own. It was put here on purpose. It's a good thing nobody got hurt."

"Oh, you think so?" Coach Renner said sarcastically.

Coach Kent stood up. "Start making sense, Renner. It was Trent's turn to go first. He's the one who would have fallen."

"Except Trent was trying to get me to take his turn, remember?" Josh gave Trent a hard look. "He said he still wasn't feeling very well. You never asked me to take your turn before, Trent."

"Do you guys alternate who goes first every day?" Otis asked.

"Yeah." Josh nodded. "Except today Trent wanted to change up. Maybe he knew about the rocky ending here."

"Oh, come on," Trent said impatiently. "I was throwing up for hours. Plus, I've been training with a terrible head cold for days."

"Too bad cell phones don't work on the mountain," Coach Kent said. "I'll go down and tell Carl to get somebody up here to take care of these rocks. I'll meet you guys at the half-pipe." He stretched and yawned. "We'll get to the bottom of this later. I want to know who's responsible."

"Maybe you *already* know." Coach Renner snorted. "It looks like you didn't get enough sleep last night. You must have been busy."

"Knock it off," the other coach muttered. "This was a nasty prank. Somebody had it in for our boys." He looked at Rae and the twins. "I'm sorry about what happened to you."

"And I'm sorry we made fun of you guys," Trent added. "You were looking good out there before you crashed. Come on over to the half-pipe with us."

"Yes, please come along," said Joshua. "I want to apologize, too. Trent and I both would have fallen if we'd hit those rocks."

"Apology accepted," said Rae. Cody and Otis nodded.

"Y'know, it's kind of hard to chill sometimes, with all the pressure," said Trent.

"Stop whining about the pressure, already," grumbled Coach Kent. "Deal with it. You're going to have to learn. What are you going to do when it's six months or two weeks until the Olympics? How about *during* the Olympics?"

The two boys nodded. "You're right," said Joshua.

The group headed over to the half-pipe, where Trent was the first to drop in. For the next couple of hours, Rae and the twins watched a dizzying bunch of backsides, frontsides, cabs, and switchbacks. They noticed that even though Trent and Joshua did lots of the same tricks, they each had a definite style.

"Joshua really gets big air," Cody said as Josh soared high up over the lip of the pipe.

"They're both super acrobatic," said Rae.

Coach Kent returned from his trip down the mountain. "Step it up, Trent," he called.

Otis couldn't take his eyes off either one of them as they did their routines. "We thought we were good, but I think they're way out of our league," he said.

Trent overheard the remark. "You guys *are* good," he said. "At least, you were pretty good on the slope-style course. Have you done the half-pipe much?"

"We've done it some," Cody answered. "We don't get the big air you guys do, though."

"We'll hang around a bit and watch you when we take a break," Trent told him.

He and Joshua kept practicing for another hour. Rae and the twins thought they were awesome. But the criticism never stopped. Both coaches constantly yelled out instructions.

"Don't drag the hand!"

"Hold on to that board!"

45

"Straighten those legs!"

"Amp it up!"

When Josh and Trent stopped for a break, the coaches each gave them a lecture about their performance.

"We're going to have to look very carefully at the variety of the tricks you're doing and the way they're placed in the routine, Josh," said his coach. "I'd like to see back-to-back nines instead of splitting them up in the run. Plus, you lost your momentum a few times. You've got to keep it smooth."

"Trent, work on your amplitude," Coach Kent told him. "You're going to have to get more air space over the lip. Hold onto the board longer in the grabs, and practice your cabs."

Cody knew that amplitude was snowboarder-speak for height, but he didn't know what a *cab* was. "What's a cab?" he asked when the coaches walked away.

Trent sat down in the snow and slipped his boots out of the bindings. "It's short for *cab-all-erial.*"

"Caballerial," Cody repeated.

"That's right, yeah. It's basically a three-sixty but you spin backward. So if you are a regular rider, you ride in fakie and spin to your left. If you are a goofy rider you would spin to . . . your right."

"There's a half-cab where you pop a one-eighty caballerial and a seven-twenty, etc.," Joshua added.

"Okay, go on, somebody drop in and show us what you've got," Trent urged.

"I'll be first," Cody said quickly. "Here goes." He dropped in and started off with an alley-oop, followed by a straight air and some spins and grabs. Rae went next, throwing down some more frontsides and backsides. They both got applause. But the one who impressed Joshua and Trent the most was Otis, who ended with a corked seven-twenty, turning his body sideways and spinning around twice in the air.

"Way to de-stroyyy it!" Trent called and whistled.

"You all have nothing to be ashamed of," said Joshua.

"Thanks. We won't be doing any competitions though." Otis pushed up his goggles. "We aren't that serious. If it isn't fun, then what's the point?"

"Wait a minute," Trent spoke up. "Just because Josh and I talk about pressure doesn't mean we aren't having fun."

"He's right," Joshua said. "If we weren't having fun, we wouldn't be doing it."

"Speaking of fun," said Cody, "I think it's time for lunch."

"Sounds good. Then maybe we should hit the weight room," said Joshua.

"You guys lift weights?" Cody asked.

"Sure we do," Trent answered. "We work out all the time. You have to be strong to do competitive snowboarding."

Otis squeezed his own arm muscle. "Maybe *we* should check out the gym while we're here. . . ."

✳

At lunch, Cody told his dad and Maxim about the rocks on the course. "The coaches said they didn't get there by accident. It looks like Otis was right. Something really weird is going on here," Cody said before biting into a hamburger. He closed his eyes. "Yum."

"This cream cheese and olive sandwich is delicious, too," said Maxim.

Cody wrinkled his nose. "*Evil olive*," he said, using another of his favorite palindromes. "I'd rather have a burger."

"Suit yourself," said Maxim. "There was quite a strong wind last night, you know. Maybe it caused some rockslides or snowslides," he said, and took another bite of his sandwich.

Otis shook his head. "I think Carl, the lift operator, put them there. He can't stand Trent and Joshua."

"Oh, Otis, I doubt that." Mr. Carson leaned toward him. "Do you really think a lift operator would risk his job, and an arrest, just to get back at some snooty guests? I don't think so."

"He's got a point," said Rae. "But then again, Carl did try really hard to convince us NOT to take the rails first—he kept telling us to start with the half-pipe."

"Hey, that's right! And Carl definitely dislikes those guys in a major way," Otis said, frowning. "You should have heard the way he talked about them. Besides, he was in the kitchen yesterday before dinner. He could have put something in that drink of Trent's."

"*If* anyone put anything in Trent's drink, he would have been taking a big chance. If he got caught he'd be fired," said Maxim.

"We have to do more investigating," said Otis.

✳

After lunch, Rae and the twins headed to the game room to play a couple of video games before going to the gym. They passed Maggie on the way. She was marching down the hall and gave a short nod of her head as she hurried by.

"Hey, Maggie, wait a second," Otis called after her. She turned and he saw that her mouth was set in a thin line.

"What is it?" she snapped, and glanced at her watch.

"Uh—I guess this isn't a g-g-good t-t-time," he stammered.

"Well, what is it? Come on, what do you want?"

Otis took a quick breath. "We were just wondering if you used a pen name. We tried to look you up online, but couldn't find you."

"We'd like to read some of your books," added Rae.

Maggie was already turning to go. "My pen name is confidential," she said sharply over her shoulder. "And I prefer not to discuss my work while I'm on vacation."

"Sheesh. She sure was in a bad mood," said Rae, when Maggie was out of earshot. "After all, *she's* the one who mentioned her bestselling books to us."

"Maybe she's just upset about something," Otis said as he raked a hand through his hair.

"She probably didn't like hearing about those rocks under the snow," Cody said.

Mrs. Crane rounded the corner quickly, and nearly bumped into them. "Oh, so sorry," she mumbled and sped on. She barely slowed down as she took something from her bag and tossed it into the trash can. Then she hustled down the hall.

Rae watched her go "Why is everyone around here in such a hurry?"

"Let's follow their example—I'll race you to the game room!" Cody challenged.

"Hold on a second," Rae said. "I stepped on something." She turned around. "Shh! Look."

Cody and Otis turned to see what she was looking at. It was Mr. Warren. He had his back to them. He dropped something into the trash can, then looked from side to side. He seemed a bit startled when he saw Rae and the twins.

"Oh, hello," he said, eyes twinkling as he gave them a big smile. "Having fun?"

"We sure are," Rae answered. The twins smiled.

"We were just going to the game room," Otis said.

"Well, have a good time," Mr. Warren said, still lingering by the garbage can.

"Come on, guys, let's go," said Rae. She turned and began walking away. The twins followed. When they neared the game room, Rae took off her shoe. A tiny pebble had lodged in the heel, and she shook it off. "Take a look—is Mr. Warren still by the garbage can?" she asked in a whisper.

"No, he's gone," said Cody.

"I want to see what he dropped into that can," said Rae. They all hurried back to the garbage can. Otis lifted off the lid, and they all peered inside. There were some papers, candy wrappers, and a few bottles. Rae reached in and picked one out. "Big Top Grape Soda," she read from the label. Then she unfolded a piece of stationery. "Maybe it's a blackmail note that wasn't delivered," she said. "Nope. This only says *Dear Uncle Ross*."

Cody reached in and pulled out a bottle. "Snap! This is Trent's bottle. The one the coach uses to make that vitamin drink. See? It's got his name on it."

The bottle was labeled **trent m**. Cody unscrewed the cap, looked inside, and sniffed. "Looks clean; smells clean." He shrugged.

Otis scratched his head. "Why would somebody wash it before throwing it out? And why throw it away here, near the elevator? Why not throw it away in the hotel room?" He rummaged around some more and pulled out another bottle. "Hmm . . . this says ipecac. I wonder what that is." He unscrewed the bottle and sniffed. "Blech! Gross! This smells awful. Smell it." He thrust it under Cody's nose.

"No, thanks!" Cody put his hand in front of his face and turned his head.

"I know what that stuff is!" Rae blurted. "My grandmother told me they used to give it to kids when they'd swallowed something they shouldn't. It made them throw up, and it smelled gross."

Otis snapped his fingers. "Remember how Maxim

told us that the maids know everything about the guests? He said they go through the trash. Whoever dumped the bottle here didn't want the maids to find the ipecac, and also didn't want them to find Trent's bottle smelling of ipecac either."

"I think you've got it, buddy," said Cody.

"It makes sense," said Rae.

"Maybe now you both will believe something crooked is going on here," Otis said.

Cody dropped the bottles back into the trash. "What's next?"

"What are you looking for in the garbage?"

They were so surprised they all jumped. Nobody had heard Mr. Warren coming up behind them.

"Uh . . . I thought m-m-my ring fell off," Rae stammered. "I threw away a candy wrapper, and then I noticed the ring was missing." She held out her hand. "But it isn't here."

Cody picked up the lid and replaced it on the can. "Let's get going," he said. "You'll probably find the ring in your room later, Rae."

"I hope so. Bye, Mr. Warren," said Rae as she and the twins turned to go. Once in the game room, she raised her hands to the sides of her face. "Ugh! He knew we were up to something."

Otis shrugged. "Well, yeah. We looked kind of strange going through the garbage."

"Who would have thought Mr. Warren would poison Trent?" Otis shook his head. "He seemed like such a nice guy."

"Slow down, cowboy," Rae said. "We don't know that it was Mr. Warren. We saw Maggie and Mrs. Crane, too. Either one of them could have put the bottles in the garbage. Or it could have been somebody else entirely."

"That's right," Cody said. "But Mrs. Crane wants Josh to have the best chance in Aspen. If Trent got sick, he couldn't train. It could throw off his performance. Don't forget what she said about Coach Renner getting older, and Josh being his last chance at Olympic coaching."

"I remember," Otis said thoughtfully. "We heard Mrs. Crane talking about Joshua's stomach trouble, too. Maybe she thought she'd even the score by giving Trent some stomach trouble of his own."

"Mr. Warren might have had the same idea," said Cody. "But what about Maggie? Why would she want to hurt Trent's chances?"

"She stands to inherit a lot of money, remember?" Rae said. "Trent could have gotten a lot worse than stomach problems. Doctors tell people not to use ipecac anymore. It's dangerous. If you take too much it can make your muscles weak, give you breathing problems, cause seizures or blackouts. It can even cause cardiac arrest."

The twins stared at her, openmouthed. "If there is a murderer here, we've got to tell the police."

"Wait a minute," Rae said. "Ipecac isn't illegal. My grandmother said people still use it as medicine."

"But it sounds like someone could *also* use it as poison." Otis shook his head. "Wow. We can't even narrow down the suspects, either. Anybody could have come along and put that stuff in the trash can. Anybody could have gone into the kitchen and poisoned Trent's drink, and anybody could have snuck out at night and put the rocks on the course. I think we're dealing with someone who is seriously dangerous."

[Chapter Seven]

 By the time Rae and the twins got to the gym, Joshua and Trent were leaving, along with their coaches. They all looked pretty angry.

"My lucky medal is missing, and you had the opportunity to steal it," Joshua said, pointing a finger at Trent.

"Get your finger out of my face."

"It could have been you," said Coach Renner, glaring at Coach Kent. "You know how much that medal means to Joshua. Maybe you wanted to get him rattled."

"It's your thinking that's rattled, Renner. I think it's nuts that Josh is superstitious about that thing, but I know lots of athletes have superstitions. They've got lucky socks, lucky coins, and even lucky underwear. But I'm not going to stoop to stealing the kid's medal. Besides, we don't need to sabotage Josh's training to do well in Aspen, do we, Trent?"

"No," Trent said through clenched teeth. "You ought to know better than that, Joshua."

"Then how come it disappeared while I was showering? I put it on the ledge in the locker room, and when I went to find it, it was gone."

"Maybe that medal *isn't* lost. Maybe you're accusing me of stealing to get me shook up," snapped Trent.

The four of them kept arguing as they brushed past Rae and the twins to leave the gym.

"Things are tense around here," said Otis, when the door had closed behind them. He saw Carl through the window. "Hey, there's Carl. Let's go talk to him."

The three ran outside. "Carl! Carl!" Otis called, waving. "Wait up."

Carl stopped and waited for Rae and the twins, who grabbed coats from hooks near the entrance and raced outside. "What do you want?" he asked, spitting the words out. He was clearly in a rotten mood.

Before anyone could answer, he held up his hand for silence. "If it's about the rocks on the course, save your breath. I would never do that. I don't like those guys, but I'm not going to try to get them hurt or lose my job. There's no way I'd go sneaking out at night to put rocks and gravel on the ground. Oscar already asked me about that, and he believes what I told him."

Rae and the twins looked at each other. Why did

Carl rush to deny that he'd done anything? Nobody had accused him.

"Do you have any idea who did it?" Otis asked.

"No. It could be almost anyone staying in the lodge. There are a lot of psychos here right now as far as I'm concerned. I like to snowboard, too, but I'm not so obsessed with winning that I'd try to hurt someone."

"We think Trent's vitamin supplement drink was tampered with, too," said Rae.

"I don't know anything about that. Those two—Trent and Joshua—are stressed out, man. Their families are stressed. Now that Oscar asked me about the rocks, *I'm* stressed, too. Look, I gotta go."

Rae and the twins watched him leave. "Do you think he's telling the truth? I'm not sure," Rae said.

"Me neither," Cody said. "Let's hit the gym."

On the way back inside they passed Mrs. Crane and Frank Warren, who were so deep in conversation they didn't even notice the three kids.

"Coach Renner is the best there is," Mrs. Crane was telling Mr. Warren. "He has a reputation for being ruthless, but he gets results. If Joshua seems a little nervous now, it doesn't matter. What he wants in his heart is to be in the Olympics. I want it for him."

"I want him to be happy, too," said Mr. Warren.

"But is Coach Renner the guy to teach good sportsmanship? He told me he'd do *anything* to win."

"Oh, come now, Frank," Mrs. Crane said with a chuckle. "He's not going to *shoot* anyone. He's just going to give it his all. He had an Olympic winner last year who retired. He knows how to get the job done. Frankly, I'm worried about that Coach Kent. He strikes me as a conniving character. No Olympic winner in three seasons. He's really hungry for a win."

"Yes, I heard him telling Trent that Joshua was the one to beat in Aspen. Then he said something like, 'If only we could get rid of him.'"

"Well, they aren't going to. I'm going to see to it that Joshua wins in Aspen. The sponsorships will start trickling in, and soon they'll be pouring in. With an Olympic gold medal, he'll be set for life with millions of dollars a year in corporate sponsorships."

Mr. Warren let out a long sigh. "I suppose that would be nice, but it's not the most important thing in life."

Mrs. Crane laughed. "Frank, you're a very nice man, but you've got a lot to learn. Money *is* the most important thing in life."

The two of them exited the building. Cody, Otis, and Rae puzzled over their conversation.

"We know that Mrs. Crane is thinking ahead to those corporate sponsorship bucks." Otis rubbed his forehead. "We also know that Coach Renner badly wants an Olympic winner. The competition in Aspen is just a step along the way, though."

"When you've got your sights on the Olympic Games, every step is important. It sure seems like Joshua, Trent, their families, and their coaches think so," said Cody.

Otis stamped his foot. "I hate this. We keep finding ourselves up blind alleys and going around and around in circles. I have this feeling that there is a clue I've overlooked. It's waiting for me to find it, but I can't." He pressed his fingers to his temples.

"Whoa there, Otis. Take it easy." Rae patted Otis on the shoulder. "We'll figure it out. We've just gotten started on this case. Something will happen that will give us the key we need."

But for the next several days, nothing *did* happen. Nothing out of the ordinary, anyway. Every day, Joshua and Trent trained. Every day, the coaches pushed and prodded them.

The tension level kept rising. Maggie fought with Mrs. Crane. "You keep trying to get Joshua more training time," she said, standing inches from Mrs.

Crane. "You keep asking the coach to show you this or that, so Joshua gets to do it over."

Mrs. Crane wasn't about to back off. "You don't frighten me," she snapped. "You're just worried that your nephew isn't doing as well as Joshua."

But that wasn't true. As the days went by, Trent got better and better, while Joshua floundered. Trent seemed to be able to take his coach's criticism and do just what he said. He amped up and got big air in the half-pipe. His cabs were smooth, and when he did a grab he held onto the board. His freestyle runs were smooth and fast.

While Trent was working on back-to-back ten-eighties in the half-pipe, Joshua couldn't get the back-to-back nines down. He fell a few times, too. His freestyle runs in the terrain park were no better. His tricks were sloppy and not as difficult as the ones Trent did. He looked more and more miserable, and his coach rode him harder and harder.

"What's the matter with you? You're falling apart. Pull yourself together!" he said after the early practice one day.

Without a word, Joshua headed for the lift. "Come back here and do it again!" Coach Renner commanded. "A winner never quits!" Joshua ignored him.

"A quitter never wins. It looks like your boy can't cut it," Coach Kent goaded the other coach. "You really think it's worth spending time on a kid like that? He crumples under pressure. Take it from me, he hasn't got it."

"Shut up!" Coach Renner growled. "I don't know if this is working out. I think Joshua and I should leave and train by ourselves somewhere else."

"Uh-oh, somebody is a little testy," Coach Kent said. A small smile played around his lips.

"Cut it out, coach," Trent said, his eyes downcast. He unfastened his rear binding, stepped out of it, and skied toward the lift.

He still looked upset when Otis saw him pacing back and forth in front of the lodge. "Want to talk, Trent?" he asked.

"Yeah, I've got to talk to somebody." Trent shoved his hands into his pockets, and together they walked toward the shed. When they got there, Trent opened the door and looked inside. "Come on in here, Otis," he said. "I don't want anyone else to hear what I have to say."

Otis followed Trent inside and sat down on a box. "What is it?"

Trent sat on another box. He didn't say anything

for a few moments. He just sat there, playing with the zipper pull on his jacket. Otis waited. Finally Trent cleared his throat and started talking.

"I've done something I shouldn't have," he said. He rolled his head back and looked at the ceiling. "Oh, man, I really shouldn't have done it." He looked at Otis. "It was so stupid, and I just did it like that." He snapped his fingers.

"I got out of the shower after lifting weights at the gym. I saw Joshua's medal on the window ledge. Josh was still in the shower, and I just picked it up and *bang*, opened my locker and threw it in my pants pocket."

"So it was you."

"Yeah, dumb old me. Josh had told me how the medal brought him luck. He believed it did, anyway. I'd been thinking he was doing a little better than I was, especially *that* day. I just picked it up and that was it."

Trent tugged his ear. "The thing is, I felt kind of good when I started showing him up . . . at first. Then I saw how upset he was, and it didn't feel so good. It went on and on, and I started to feel that I was cheating. I didn't want to be better that way."

"So apologize and give the medal back to him," Otis said.

Trent sighed. "I want him to have it back, believe

me. But he would never trust me again. He'd be really angry, too. I've learned my lesson, and I'll never do anything like that again. But if I tell Josh what I did, we will never be friends again, ever. It could also get me kicked off the team."

Otis thought for a moment. He liked Trent, and he wanted to believe him. He decided to help him out.

"Give me the medal. I'll say I found it, and I'll give it back to Joshua."

"Really? Awesome." Trent handed Otis the medal. He was wearing a big smile.

Otis held the medal in his hand. It had a picture of a snowboarder sailing down a mountain and a large number one. He hoped he was right to trust Trent.

∗

That night, Otis caught up with Joshua after dinner. He was on his way outside and had just pulled his hood up over his short blond hair. Otis tapped him on the shoulder. "Can we talk for a minute?"

Joshua shrugged. "Sure. What's up?"

Otis pulled the medal from his pocket. "I found something that belongs to you. It was under the radiator in the gym. I saw it when I bent down to take off my shoe." He put the medal into Joshua's gloved hand.

Joshua stared at it. "How is that possible? I looked everywhere. The cleaning staff were told to be on the lookout for it."

"Well, that's how it happens sometimes, isn't it? Everyone looks all over the place for something, and then it just turns up. I've seen it happen before, and I can never figure it out. I'm just glad I could give it back to you."

"Yeah, thanks," Joshua said softly. He looked Otis in the eye and held his gaze for a moment. Then he headed out into the night, pulling his ski mask down over his nose and mouth to protect them from the cold. He liked to walk by himself when it was dark and he could look up at the stars. He clutched the medal tightly in his hand before putting it in the pocket of his jacket.

He felt something in the pocket that didn't belong to him. He pulled it out and studied it in the moonlight. It was a pack of cough drops, but he hadn't bought any cough drops. He searched the other pocket and pulled out a candy bar that didn't belong to him, either. He realized that, after dinner, he had grabbed Trent's jacket from a coat hook by mistake. It was the last thought he had before he felt something hit him in the head, hard. Then he passed out.

[Chapter Eight]

When Joshua woke up it was dark and cold. He didn't know where he was—at first. Then his eyes focused on the stars, and he looked out into the vast open space. He felt the metal chair underneath him. He realized that he was on the ski lift. What was he doing on the ski lift?

He rubbed his aching head. When he took his hand away, the fingers of his glove were wet with blood. Someone must have hit him and sent his unconscious body up on the ski lift.

Joshua knew he didn't have time to wonder who had hit him and why. He had to get down and back to the lodge immediately. But there was a serious problem with that. He couldn't just step off the lift. He figured that the lift had been stopped when the chair was about fifteen feet above the ground—except for the part that was suspended over a ravine, which was most of it. His stomach lurched. His fingers were nearly numb even through his gloves.

Joshua knew he had to figure out how to get down to the jutting lip of ground without falling backward into the ravine. *I'm too cold to think!*

As soon as the thought entered his mind he pushed it away. He hadn't gotten to where he was as a snowboarder by giving up. He had a chance to be an Olympic contender, and he wasn't about to give that up without a fight. The only way to avoid being overcome by fear was to focus on saving himself.

He didn't dare jump. Even if he jumped off the back of the chair, he might miss the lip of ground— or hit it and slide into the ravine. The noise of the uncontrollable chattering of his teeth was like a frantically beating drum in his head. He rubbed his frozen fingers together.

Seconds ticked by as he focused on the problem the way he focused on his snowboarding. He shut out everything else. Then, he knew what he had to do. First, he pulled the medal from his coat pocket and stuffed it down into his sock. Then he started taking off his clothes.

He tied the sleeve of his coat to the chair frame, making a tight knot. Then he pulled his pants down over his boots and tied a leg to the other coat sleeve. He had on long thermal underwear underneath.

In spite of the warm gloves he wore, Joshua's fingers were getting stiffer and stiffer. He had to work fast. So far he had created a little over six feet of "rope." He needed more. After he pulled off his hoodie and sat on it, he added his thermal top to the rope. Now he had about nine feet of fabric to climb.

His whole body shivered with cold. Balancing carefully on the seat of the chairlift, he pulled the hoodie back on over his bare chest and pulled the hood up over his throbbing head. His fingers fumbled as he knotted the drawstring at his neck.

Joshua decided he'd have to take a chance on jumping when he reached the end of the "rope." He was wearing his hoodie, his long underwear pants, gloves, face mask, socks, and boots. Frostbite would surely be a danger if he removed anything else.

Joshua threw the clothing rope off the chair. Then he climbed out of the chair and began to lower himself down. He tried his best to grip the rope tightly, but he could hardly feel his hands. Little by little, he began to edge his way down.

A slight wind had been blowing, but now it kicked

up and a gust sent the rope sailing out over the ravine. It swayed back, then out again, then back. Joshua shut his eyes tightly. Then the rope steadied and he forced himself to begin climbing down again. His hands felt like blocks of ice at the ends of his wrists.

He was nearing the end. Joshua figured he had to jump about ten feet. He was sure he could do that much without getting hurt. The snow was deep and would give him a cushion to land on. He told himself that he was going to make it.

The wind kicked up again, blowing toward the ravine. Joshua was so surprised that he lost his grip on the rope. He was free-falling in the air, dangerously close to the edge of land. He squeezed his eyes shut once more, then hit the ground with a muffled *thud*. His heart lurched. He was safe on the ground . . . but only for a moment.

He had landed near the edge of the lip that jutted over the ravine. Another gust of wind blew him farther toward the edge. The ground sloped downward, and Joshua found himself sliding toward the ravine. He reached out wildly but there was nothing to clutch onto, only handfuls of snow.

The wind pushed him farther and farther. His feet

hung over the ledge, then his knees . . . and then his whole body was over the edge, and he was hanging onto the lip of land desperately.

Suddenly the wind stopped and the air was still. Joshua fumbled in the snow with his fingers and found a piece of rock underneath it. He grabbed it as tightly as he could while he reached forward slowly with his other hand. He found another rock. He held onto them as if his life depended on it . . . and it did.

Joshua's arms were freezing but on fire with the exertion of wrenching himself up. Finally he dared to swing one leg up to solid ground. He gritted his teeth and refused to give in to the pain in his arms as he scrambled to his feet. When he was out of danger, he lay down on the snow, breathing heavily until he was able to sit up.

Now that he was no longer dangling over the edge of a ravine, a heavy wave of fatigue swept over him. His eyes closed, and he thought of how tired he was. A feeling of drowsy warmth seeped into his veins. How nice it would be to stay right where he was and drift off to sleep, he thought.

If I do that, I'll die! The thought screamed into his head. He had heard about lost travelers who fell asleep in the snow. Somehow he hauled himself to his feet.

He began to walk. He saw the lights of the lodge in the distance—he judged that it must be about a mile away, but with fatigue and cold drilling through him, it might as well have been twenty miles.

As he walked, the lights appeared to move farther away with every step. His brain was starting to play delirious tricks on him—for a minute, he believed that he was riding his snowboard in the Olympics, in a race he was losing. Then he thought he had his first dog with him, though she had died two years ago. He knew he was running out of time.

Somehow Joshua kept going. In spite of the cold, his eyelids grew heavier and heavier. Several times he started to fall asleep. But the medal he'd put in his sock kept digging into his ankle as he walked. The sharp pain kept him awake, and it saved his life.

Finally he reached the lodge and opened the door. The clerk was so upset when he saw the bloodied, frozen figure that he screamed as he came running out from behind the desk. That roused the guests who were sitting in the lobby. They all got up and hurried to see what was going on.

Joshua staggered a few steps and tugged off the hoodie and face mask. He took a few deep breaths, and then collapsed. There were loud gasps from the guests. "Joshua!" his mother cried as she ran to him. Frank Warren hurried after her. Rae and the twins saw the color drain from his face.

Everyone crowded around Joshua. His face was blue from the cold, and there was clotted blood on his head. He opened his eyes and tried to say something.

"Shh, keep quiet, take it easy," the clerk told him. Then he called an ambulance.

"What happened?" Frank Warren asked the clerk urgently. His eyes were wild and he seemed out of his mind with worry.

"I don't know," he said as he pushed his spectacles up on his nose. "I guess he was out walking and fell down." Rae and the twins exchanged glances. Otis shook his head.

$$*$$

"Joshua didn't fall down," Otis said later, after Josh had been taken away in the ambulance. "Somebody hurt him, I just know it. I'll bet when he wakes up he'll tell someone, and the police will be here first thing tomorrow."

But the following morning they walked into the dining room and found everyone acting as if nothing unusual had happened. "Look, Mrs. Crane and Frank

Warren are talking and eating their muffins as if they didn't have a worry in the world," said Otis.

"*Sniff 'um, muffins*," Cody muttered.

"Think of something besides palindromes, Cody," hissed Rae.

"Yeah," Otis seconded, "let's see if we can find out what's going on."

The three of them approached the table. "We've been worried about Joshua," said Otis. "What happened to him? Is he all right?"

Mrs. Crane and Mr. Warren both smiled. "Thank you for asking. Joshua will be fine. It was lucky he wasn't far from the lodge. He must have fallen and hit his head. Then the cold made him delirious enough to remove some of his clothes."

"I've heard about that happening when people get lost in the cold," said Rae.

"I don't see how he could have gotten lost, but he was out in the cold for hours. The doctors said he's lucky—he just has a little frostbite. He'll be out of the hospital today and back to training soon. There was no concussion, but he can't remember a thing that happened after he went out for his walk."

[Chapter Nine]

Joshua came back to the lodge the same day that Otis spoke to Mrs. Crane about the accident. Two days later, he was back to training. Rae and the twins asked him about what happened a few times, but he couldn't remember. Since their investigation was going nowhere, they spent their time doing tricks in the terrain park and watching Joshua and Trent train.

"Anyone else feel like going for a ride?" Rae asked one morning.

Cody and Otis liked the idea. They all grabbed their freeride boards, which were longer and wider than their freestyle boards, and headed out. They traveled beyond the half-pipe and into the freeride area.

"Let's keep going," Cody urged when Rae and Otis wanted to start down the mountain. "We haven't seen any signs or warning tape, and the scenery keeps getting better."

Rae and Otis had to agree. Finally they stopped at three large boulders and looked down. Before them was a breathtaking, clean expanse of smooth, sparkling snow. "It would be awesome to ride that," said Cody.

"Let's go," Rae said eagerly. She pushed off. The twins followed.

They soared along the snow. It felt like flying. The clear blue sky seemed so near that they could touch it.

Then suddenly they all heard a *boom!* It turned into a roar that kept on rumbling. A word screamed into their minds: *avalanche!*

They instantly began streaking to the side of the slope in desperation, racing as fast as they could go. They all felt their hearts hammering wildly in their chests. All three of them had been drilled over and over in avalanche safety by their snowboarding instructor and by Maxim. Most important was to try to get out of the way of the avalanche, not to outrun it.

Outrunning an avalanche was impossible. The slabs of snow traveled as fast as two hundred miles an hour. Survival depended on split-second reaction.

The wild rumbling and roaring pounded their eardrums. Cody, Otis, and Rae were all having trouble with the second rule of avalanche survival: Don't panic.

Cody pointed his board down the side of the slope

as he worked an emergency breathing tube into his mouth, just in case he got buried.

Otis's stomach was doing flip-flops, but he tried to keep his mind blank. His whole body had switched into overdrive.

Rae fought to keep from squeezing her eyes shut. She was unaware that she was biting her lip so hard it was bleeding.

The monstrous, thundering snow created its own wind as it sucked everything into its path—trees, rocks, earth. Otis, Cody, and Rae felt the force of it and swayed on their boards.

Then, just as they were certain they weren't going to make it, the gigantic cascade flashed past them. The edge of it almost grazed Cody's board. The force of the hurling snow whirled them all around as it went rumbling down the mountain.

They stopped, breathless and panting, their lungs crying for air. Otis leaned over and put his hands on his knees, weak with relief. It was then that he saw a figure tumbling over and over in the wall of snow below.

"The avalanche got somebody," he wheezed. "I think it was a guy. He's going to be buried alive!"

It had all happened so fast—it took less than a

minute for tons of snow to hurtle down the mountain. Then all was quiet, and an eerie stillness took the place of the rumble and roar.

Rae was trembling, and Cody could feel his knees shaking. "That was a close one," he said.

"You're not kidding," Otis panted. He stood up straight. "We've got to help that guy," he said. "We don't have much time."

The three of them checked to make sure that their avalanche beacons were set on "receive," turned up the volume, and started making their way down the mountain. They all hoped the avalanche victim was wearing a beacon and safety breathing device, too.

Without the breathing device, you could stay alive for about fifteen minutes under the snow. That is, if you had somehow kept a space in front of your face to breathe. Even then, you might be so tightly packed in snow that you couldn't expand your lungs. Snow is heavy, and in an avalanche you could be buried under twenty feet or more. Even if your location was found right away, there wouldn't be time to dig you out.

An avalanche safety breathing device buys you time by drawing in oxygen from the snowpack. You breathe in through a tube in your mouth. The carbon dioxide is pushed out a vent at the base of your spine and into the snow. A breathing device could increase your ability to last under the snow to thirty to forty-five minutes . . . maybe even an hour. *It was the difference between life and death.*

Was the trapped person wearing a beacon? Did he have a breathing device? If Rae and the twins could even find him, how deeply was he buried? Was he badly hurt? Would they be able to dig him out? They raced down the mountain, each of them fearing the risk of a second avalanche.

"Do you hear that?" Otis stopped suddenly. "My beacon is beeping."

"Mine, too," said Rae and Cody at the same time.

"Let's go," said Otis.

They began gliding across the signal area. They noted where the signal was strongest and where it ended. They marked the points with whatever they could find—a piece of tree branch, or a rock.

Soon they were able to pinpoint the place where the signal was stronger. All took out portable probing poles and snapped them into full length. They began shoving them into the snow at forty-five degree angles, which they knew was the best way to avoid disturbing an air pocket.

"If we don't find him soon, one of us should go and get help," said Cody, shoving his pole into the snow.

Just then they heard garbled noises coming from under the snow. "I think he's only three or four feet under," said Rae. "That sure is lucky." She pulled a portable shovel from her backpack. Cody and Otis did the same.

They all began shoveling as fast as they could. The snow was packed tightly, and it was slow going. Every once in a while they would hear the garbled voice from under the snow again.

They were all sweating and aching from the exertion. Finally, they were close enough to hear something that sounded like, "I'm here!" loud enough to know they were close. Rae began digging in the snow with her hands. She uncovered the eyes first, then the nose, then the mouth holding a breathing tube. They all stared in shock.

It was Trent Margolis.

Rae and the twins began shoveling again. They were able to free Trent's hands and arms. Then he could help a little with the digging.

Trent removed the breathing tube from his mouth. "I don't think I'm hurt, except for some bruises. I'm sure glad you guys were around."

"So are we," said Otis. "We're all glad we weren't buried, too."

"I barely escaped it," said Cody. "The heavy stuff

was almost to the edge of my board. It was my lucky day, too."

After a shoveling frenzy by Rae and the twins, most of the snow was cleared away.

"Make sure nothing's broken," said Cody. "Nothing feels loose, does it?"

Trent felt his legs, ankles, and arms. "I think I'm okay." With the help of the twins, he was able to rise to a wobbly stance. "Whoa!" he said as he put a hand on Cody's shoulder to steady himself. "I'd better go to a hospital and get checked out just in case."

"Definitely," said Cody.

They had all been so focused on digging that they hadn't noticed snow had begun to fall from the sky. Now it started to fall thicker and faster.

Trent did a couple of squats. "I'll be okay to get back to the lodge," he said. "We'd better get off this mountain. It sure feels like a storm is coming."

Cody and Otis nodded and prepared to take off.

Rae hesitated a moment. "What did it feel like, Trent?"

Trent ran a hand over his face. "Wow, let me think. Maybe like being hit by a collapsing brick wall while you're in the middle of a tornado."

[Chapter Ten]

By the time Rae and the twins arrived back at the lodge with Trent, the snow was tumbling down.

"There was an avalanche," Cody announced to the group in the lobby. "We were freeriding in the back country up the mountain," he said. "I was almost caught in it, and Trent got trapped, but we found him and dug him out."

Everyone was murmuring, "Thank goodness," and "You just never know," and "Very lucky young man," except for Coach Kent. He was giving Trent a steely stare. "What were you doing in the back country?"

"It wasn't in the part that was sectioned off with tape, and we didn't see any signs," said Cody.

Rae nodded. "I kept thinking I'd see something, but I never did."

"How far did you go? Can you describe the place?" Coach Kent asked.

"We basically went west of the pipe for about an hour," Otis began. "Near the top of the slope there were these three big boulders. . . ."

Oscar's eyes opened wide. "What?! You were near the three boulders? That's definitely in the off-limits area. How could you not see any signs? How could you not see the yellow warning tape?"

"Because they weren't there," Rae said firmly.

"Oh no, no." Oscar put his head in his hands. "Someone took down the signs and the tape. How could anyone do something so dangerous?"

Coach Kent's expression hadn't changed. "What happened to the signs, Trent?" he demanded.

"Well, *I* didn't take them," Trent said, looking his coach in the eye. "And I *didn't* start the avalanche."

"I'll bet *someone* did!" Cody said.

"Oh, no, no, Cody. There was nothing scheduled for today," Oscar said. "You see, sometimes rangers set off charges to cause an avalanche deliberately. That way it won't happen accidentally. I would know if they were going to do that."

Cody shook his head. "But we heard this gigantic *boom!* right before the avalanche started. It was like dynamite exploding."

"It was an explosion all right," Otis agreed.

"A really, really *big* explosion," said Rae.

Oscar clasped his hands in front of his chest. "Yes, yes, that is *exactly* what an avalanche sounds like. Avalanches make all kinds of noises—you didn't hear any dynamite, I'm sure of that."

Cody and Otis exchanged glances. They were sure it *had* been dynamite.

Mr. Warren's frown was becoming deeper and deeper. "Maybe there was no dynamite. But somebody removed those signs and the tape. Who did that, and why didn't the ski patrol do something about it?"

Mrs. Crane had been standing there silently, her lips pressed tightly together. "This is just ridiculous!" she snapped. "Joshua could have been the one in that avalanche. He might have died."

Oscar held up his hands for silence. "Please, everyone, we all know that this is serious. But we must keep calm. Obviously, someone removed the signs shortly before you kids arrived."

Coach Renner patted Mrs. Crane on the arm. "Don't worry. Everything will be all right."

"It will be all right when we get out of here and Joshua is safe, and that will be soon," said Mr. Warren.

"Yes, our group is leaving, too," said Maxim. "I'm sorry, Oscar. It isn't your fault. It's just that the situation here right now has a distinctly bad vibe."

Oscar's frame drooped. "I'm so sorry, everyone. But

I'm afraid you won't be able to leave just yet. You see, there is a severe storm warning in this area, and the avalanche has blocked the road completely. The storm is only going to get worse."

He was right. They all looked outside and saw what appeared to be a thick, white curtain. Heavy gusts were whirling the snow into clouds, and the trees were swaying. The wind was a menacing howl.

"One more thing." Oscar cleared his throat. "The avalanche knocked the phones out."

There was a chorus of groans in the room.

"I'm so sorry," said Oscar. "Free desserts for everyone tonight."

"Well, that's the first good thing that's happened today!" quipped Cody. "I'm going for the triple chocolate cake. *No lemons, no melon.*"

Rae rolled her eyes. "Only *you* could dream up a palindrome at a time like this!"

"I solve crimes better on a full stomach," said Cody to Rae as they entered the dining room. "We can talk about the case at the table."

But Mr. Carson vetoed that plan. "Let's not have any talk of crime during the meal," he said firmly. "I want to eat dinner in peace."

✳

By the time they finished dinner, the snow had stopped falling, but the wind still howled viciously. Mr. Carson paid for the meal with his credit card. The waiter glanced at the tip as he picked up the receipt. "Thank you, sir." He smiled.

At a nearby table, where Mrs. Crane and Mr. Warren sat, another waiter was picking up a credit card receipt. "Wow, thank you, sir!" he said, beaming at Mr. Warren.

He showed the receipt to another waiter. "That guy always gives great tips," he said. "Not like that other deadbeat." He nodded toward Coach Kent. "Not a dime, do you believe that? I wouldn't trust somebody who never left a tip." The other waiter nodded.

The guests began getting up from their tables and wandering into the lobby.

"Winds like this rip the trees right out of the ground," said Maggie as she gazed out at the storm. "We've got to get out of here. It's awful being cooped up with a murderer." She looked directly at Coach Renner, who turned away.

"Honestly, Maggie," said Maxim. "No one has been murdered. Come and sit down. What on earth are you talking about?"

When they were seated around a table in the corner, Maggie glanced sideways across the room at

Coach Renner before she started to speak. "I've heard things about him. They're just rumors, of course. But I've heard that one reason he wins so often is that he'll do anything to win."

"We've heard that before," said Cody. "*Anything* meant anything he could do to train a snowboarder to win."

Maggie shook her head impatiently. "That's what *he* says. Other people say that he's done some dangerous things. He arranged for an opponent of his client to have an 'accident.' His car's brakes failed, and he was in the hospital for months. There were other things, too. They say he's thrown games—paid off opponents to lose."

Rae, Cody, and Otis were taking this all in. Their minds were busy coming up with ideas. Could what she was saying be true?

"As you said, Maggie, these are just rumors," Maxim reminded her. "Frankly, such a successful coach might have some enemies among the jealous, you know."

Maggie leaned back and let out a long sigh. "I had a feeling you wouldn't believe me. Now we're trapped here with him, and I'm worried about Trent."

"Things are so tense around here that everyone is getting carried away. Someone may decide to take vengeance for an imagined crime." said Maxim, stretching out his long legs and crossing his ankles.

Maggie sat up and tilted her head back. "I suppose so, but Coach Renner already has a grudge against Kent. And if the coach was out of the picture, Trent's performance would suffer. Don't forget, Coach Renner is getting older."

"So therefore he is desperate to have an Olympic athlete to coach now?" Maxim shook his head. "You're reaching, Maggie. He doesn't seem like a desperate man to me; he seems like a determined one. So does Coach Kent. Both are competitive. But if Coach Renner were trying to knock out the competition, I think he'd go right for Trent himself." Maxim smiled at Rae and the twins. "Your sleuthing is rubbing off. I'm becoming a bit of a detective."

Later, Cody, Otis, and Rae went to the game room to talk things over. "Our villain is right here under our noses," said Cody. "The trouble is, right now everyone except the three of us, and Dad and Maxim, of course, are suspects. Think about it. Everybody has a motive."

"I'm wondering if there might be more than one villain," said Rae. "I wish Joshua could remember what happened the night of his accident."

[Chapter Eleven]

"We keep running into roadblocks," Cody said glumly.

"I know something we might try," said Rae. "It's risky, though."

"How risky?" Cody asked. He shifted in his seat.

"Oh, don't worry so much," Otis snorted. "What's your idea, Rae?"

"Well, you know I've been reading about avalanches. Like Oscar said, ski patrols often set off charges to cause avalanches deliberately. When they explode, the dynamite leaves a huge hole in the ground called a bomb crater. We could go up to the place where the avalanche started and look for a crater. That's how we'd know if the avalanche was caused on purpose."

"Uh, wait a minute," Cody said, holding up his hand. "I think *risky* is an understatement. What if there's another avalanche?"

"Aw, Cody, relax." Otis replied. He stood up. "You just heard that they cause avalanches to stop them from happening out of nowhere. The avalanche already happened."

"I still think we should be careful. After all, that area is officially off-limits."

"All right, so we'll be careful," Otis said. "Can we find the bomb crater under the snow?"

"I think so," said Rae. "There will still be a big hole, even if it's covered with snow. I'll bet we can find it . . . if it's there."

"Of course, if we find it we can't tell anybody without admitting we went right where we weren't supposed to go," said Cody.

Otis plopped down on a couch, leaned back, and crossed his legs. "We'll worry about that problem when we come to it," he said.

*

The next morning at breakfast, Rae and the twins were anxious. They didn't want to leave Colorado before they'd solved this case. They were relieved when Maxim said that there was no word about clearing the avalanche. "No phone service yet," he told them.

"We might as well make the best of it," Rae said, flashing a smile that was a little too large. "When you're given lemons you've gotta make lemonade, right? Let's get some more snowboarding in."

"I'm with you, Rae," Otis said, grinning.

"Sure," Cody chimed in.

Mr. Carson put down his fork. "I'm not so sure that's a good idea," he said. "Maybe it isn't safe."

Oscar was passing by their table and overheard. "Excuse me, Mr. Carson, but it *is* safe to go snowboarding. My staff has been grooming the trails and the terrain park since early this morning. The lift is running. Let the young people enjoy themselves while they are here."

"There isn't much else we can do, Dad," Otis said quietly. He glanced around the room. "Where is everybody?" The tables were nearly empty.

Oscar sighed. "The Crane group and the Margolis group ordered room service. That way they won't have to see each other in the dining room."

"Have they gone up on the lift yet?" Rae asked.

"I don't think so," answered Oscar. He looked at Maxim. "I'm so sorry, my old friend, that your visit has been spoiled."

Maxim put down his napkin and shook his head. "It's most unfortunate, but the things that have happened aren't your fault. We'll be back, won't we, Hayden?"

Mr. Carson glanced up at Oscar. "Oh, of course we'll be back," he said, but he didn't sound too sure.

"We promise to be extra careful, Dad," said Cody.

Mr. Carson looked doubtful. Rae and the twins stared at him, eagerly waiting for the answer they wanted.

"Oh, all right," he said finally.

"Thank you!" said Rae with a huge smile. Otis and Cody bolted from the table.

"Let's get dressed and grab our boards," said Otis as soon as they were outside the dining room. He looked down the hallway and tilted his head to one side. "There's Josh—it looks like something's wrong." They hurried to catch up with Joshua, who was frowning and rubbing the back of his head.

"How's it goin', Josh?" asked Cody, walking beside him.

"Hi, guys," Joshua said, nodding to Rae and the twins. "I had this really weird dream about the accident when I hurt my head. It kind of freaked me out."

Rae and the twins held their breath. Did the dream trigger a memory?

"I heard someone come up behind me just before I got hit on the head. Then I saw myself waking up on the ski lift, freezing to death, with no idea how I got there. I know this sounds crazy, but in the dream I tied some of my clothes together to get down from the ski lift—because it was too far to jump. Then I was walking through the snow—walking and walking and walking." He shuddered. "It was so cold."

"Well, maybe that's what really happened," said Rae carefully. "Maybe that was a memory, not a dream."

Joshua gritted his teeth. "Nah, I think it's just the stress of getting ready to compete. It's too weird. Nobody would hit me on the head and haul me up on a ski lift. It was just a nightmare."

"What if it really happened, and the person who did it is still here?" prodded Cody.

Joshua shoved his hands in his pockets and began to walk faster. "I don't want to talk about this anymore. I'm stressed enough about training and competing. Nobody here would try to kill me."

"We think they would," Otis said under his breath. "That was no nightmare—I bet it's exactly what happened." They watched Joshua walk away and decided not to go after him. Maybe he'd be ready to talk more about it later. For now, they'd concentrate on another part of their investigation.

✳

"Where's Carl?" Cody asked Mike, who was operating the chairlift.

"Somebody stole a snowmobile, and they've got a load of people looking for it all over the mountain," he said. "It's not one of ours," he added. "It's from one of the other lodges."

The chair hit the backs of their legs. Cody, Otis, and Rae took a seat.

"Have fun, and stay safe," Mike called to them as the lift began moving up the mountain.

"I wonder who stole the snowmobile," Rae said, pulling on her gloves.

"I'll bet it's somebody who wanted to go joy-riding," Cody said. He inhaled deeply. "This mountain air is great. It's good in the mountains near home, too, but this smells different."

"It sure is beautiful up here," said Otis. It was a bright day and the mountain was bathed in glittering sunlight. The trees stood tall and proud against the sky. Broken branches appeared here and there, evidence of the previous night's raging winds.

"I wish we could stay longer," said Rae wistfully. Then her face brightened. "If we find the culprit, maybe we can."

"Maybe," said Cody. "I just hope it isn't Trent or Joshua or one of their coaches."

"Well, it's going to be *somebody*," said Otis. "Anyway, heads up, it's time to get off the lift."

An operator who introduced himself as Ben held the chair while they hopped off. They moved away from the lift and stepped into their bindings. Trent waved at them from the entrance to the terrain park. "You guys coming in?"

"Nah, we're going to freeride for a while," said Cody. "Maybe we'll see you later."

"Trent and Josh are still training together," Otis observed.

They rode toward the freestyle area, and then passed it by on the way to the back country. Several signs warning them to go no farther were posted along the way.

"Did we really go this far?" Rae asked after a while.

"Yeah, we have to reach the spot with the three boulders, remember?" Otis glided along the snow. They passed another warning sign and then ducked under the yellow tape that had been tied around the trees. "We're getting close now."

Then suddenly Otis had a tingling feeling on the back of his neck. A little shiver ran along his spine. He slowed and waited for Cody to move alongside him.

"I know, and I feel it, too," said his brother. At times they shared feelings and didn't need words to explain them. It had happened for as long as they could remember. A feeling would come over them suddenly, out of nowhere, and somehow they knew they shared it.

"What's going on?" Rae asked. "You guys look like you've seen a ghost."

"We're being watched," Cody whispered. "Shh."

They all stood as still as statues. Their ears strained for the slightest sound, and their eyes scanned the trees for movement. But there was not so much as the crack of a twig or the rustle of branches.

"We might as well get going," said Cody. He began gliding across the snow again.

"I can see the three boulders up ahead," said Otis. "We ought to start looking for that crater."

They heard the whir of a snowmobile. Then they caught sight of it flying over the snow. "Hey!" Cody called out.

The snowmobile slowed to a stop. The rider got off and raised his goggles. It was Carl.

"What are you guys doing out here? Can't you see all the signs and the tape? We were out here early this morning putting them up. Yesterday you said you didn't know any better, but today you do."

Cody and Otis exchanged glances. They didn't want to tell Carl what they were looking for. He was still a suspect. They couldn't risk letting him know they were looking for evidence.

"What are *you* doing out here, Carl?" Rae challenged.

"I'm looking for the stolen snowmobile," Carl said in his sulky voice. "If I find it, I've got to get somebody up here to get it down. I'd like to find whoever stole it, too, and take 'em down the mountain."

"One of us could take the snowmobile back," Cody volunteered. "We all know how to ride them."

"Not a chance," said Carl. "If somebody gets hurt riding it, there's trouble. The place will get sued, big-time." He got back on the snowmobile. "You guys get right back to the terrain park," he said, "and I won't tell anybody I saw you. But get going."

"Okay, Carl," said Otis.

"Nice of him to say he wouldn't tell on us," Rae remarked when Carl had gone.

"I think if he were guilty of something, he would have stayed around to make sure we left," said Cody. "He would've acted more suspicious. Don't you think so, Otis?"

Otis shrugged. "Yeah, I guess. But it's hard to tell how Carl thinks. Let's keep hunting for the crater."

As they continued along, Otis still had that tingling feeling of being watched. He knew that Cody did, too. It kept getting stronger and stronger.

"Hey, I think I found the crater," Rae called from up ahead. "It's huge."

The twins rode up and stopped beside Rae. She had stepped off her board and was standing beside an enormous circular bowl several feet deep in the snow. It was where they figured the avalanche had started. The twins unstrapped their boards so that they could walk up to the crater.

"Well, it doesn't look natural, that's for sure," said Cody. "But how do we know it was made by dynamite?"

"Dynamite would leave residue behind," Rae said, sitting down in the snow. She took the portable shovel from her backpack and slid to the edge of the crater. She dug scoopfuls of snow from part of the bowl.

"Do you need help?" Otis asked.

Rae kept shoveling. "I don't think so. How deep do you guys think the snowfall was?"

"Maybe a couple of feet," Otis answered.

Rae held up her shovel. "Look at this."

There was a coating of sticky black goop on the edge of her shovel. "I read that this is what dynamite leaves behind," she said. "So it *was* dynamite that we heard." She sniffed. "It smells bad, too."

Otis went over and took a whiff. "Ugh. It's like dirty smoke," he said.

Rae took a rag from her backpack and wiped the

shovel clean. She folded the rag carefully and placed it in her backpack with the shovel. "Evidence," she said, and snapped photos of the crater with her phone.

"Yeah, but how are we going to let anyone know about it?" Cody asked. He shifted from one foot to the other.

"We'll think of something," Otis said. "We'll have to. There is someone out here who set off the dynamite. That's a pretty important thing for the ski patrol to know."

"But what if it tips off the criminal?" Rae asked.

Otis sighed. "We can't think about that now. We'll figure something out when we get back to the lodge." He looked around and shook himself. "I still feel like we're being watched."

"It's creepy," said Cody. "Let's get out of here."

They all stepped into their snowboard bindings and started back, searching for a movement or a sound that would signal someone in hiding. There was only the soft *whoosh* of their boards gliding on the snow.

Suddenly they heard branches rustling. There was a low, rumbling growl. An animal stepped into the clearing.

The cougar stood still, lowered its head, and stared at them with golden eyes. It wasn't the size that was the most fearsome thing about it. It was the power in the muscles under its tawny coat. It was the way it gathered itself like a coiled spring. Most of all, it was the predatory look in its eyes.

Rae and the twins knew that there was something wrong with this cougar—there had to be. A cougar wouldn't step into a clearing in front of its prey. It would spring up from behind . . . and go for the back of the neck.

Cody glanced at his brother. Otis had a kind of magic with animals. It had saved them from being charged by a wild boar in the Amazon jungle. Would it work now on a wounded cougar?

Otis stood so still that he looked as if he had been turned to ice. He stared the cougar right in the eye, his gaze unwavering. If the magic was going to happen, he and the animal would begin to communicate without words. But he saw a huge gash on the cougar's side, from its shoulder to its flank. The wound looked badly infected. This animal was very sick.

Time slowed to a crawl for Cody, Otis, and Rae. Sweat beaded on their foreheads. Their hearts hammered in their chests, and their minds exploded with fear. It took every ounce of effort they had to control their panic and not race away as fast as they could.

They all knew that no matter how much they wanted to, that was the worst thing they could do. Speeding away could trigger an attack. The cougar didn't move. Still staring at them intently, the big cat lowered its hundred-pound body into a crouch. Its tail twitched back and forth, its ears erect. Then it began pumping its hind legs up and down.

The magic is not going to happen, Otis thought. *The cougar is out of its mind with pain. I can't reach it. It's going to attack any second now.* Otis wondered which one of them the big cat would pounce on first. If it was him, he would try to fight with his bare hands. He would try to go for the eyes . . . if he could.

It's time now, a voice whispered in Otis's head. He knew the same voice was whispering to Cody. From the corner of his eye, he could see Rae's body tense as she steeled herself for the attack.

The cougar growled again.

It's going to be me, Otis realized. He was sure of it.

The big cat crouched lower, its eyes boring into Otis. It gathered its body into a mass of coiled energy and began to launch itself into a mighty spring. . . .

Bang! The sound of a gunshot ripped through the air.

[Chapter Twelve]

The cougar froze. Cody, Otis, and Rae watched, gripped in shock. Another shot rang out. The cougar gave the three of them a parting glance, and trotted into the trees. Its gait was halting and clumsy. It didn't look as if it would get far.

"Who's there?" Cody called out shakily. "Thank you for helping us!"

"Who are you?" Otis yelled.

There was no answer.

"Hello?" Rae shouted.

Nobody called to them. No one came forward.

Finally, they started back toward the lift.

When they neared the terrain park, they saw that Trent and Joshua were still training. Trent was going over a rail, and he looked really good. Joshua and the two coaches stood on the sidelines watching. Music was playing in the background, a fast pulsing beat.

"I don't think they heard the shots, so let's not say anything unless they bring it up," said Cody.

"Right," said Otis. "We won't have to explain where we were to anybody . . . unless Carl says something."

"If they mention the gunfire, we'll tell them we heard it from far away," Rae said.

At the ski lift, they were relieved when Mike, the operator, didn't say anything about the shots. "Carl was here just a little while ago. He said they found that missing snowmobile."

"Where?" Otis asked as he sat in the chair. Cody and Rae climbed in beside him.

"Well, it's the weirdest thing." Mike shook his head as he steadied the chairlift. "Whoever stole it snuck it back to the lodge while everybody was out looking for it. Pretty slick, right?"

"Yeah," Otis agreed. "Listen, just now I think we saw a badly wounded cougar. It was just beyond the off-limits area. I don't think it'll live very long."

Mike's eyes narrowed. "Tell Oscar or one of the workers when you get to the lodge. They can have an animal patrol sent out. Maybe they can help it."

As the lift began to move, Rae scowled.

Cody watched her. "What are you thinking?"

"Oh." Rae gave her head an impatient shake. "I thought that I had this thing all figured out, and Carl was the guilty one," she said. "He was in the kitchen the day Trent got sick. He doesn't like him, and maybe he poisoned the drink. And he could have been the one who trapped Joshua on the lift."

"It sounds right so far. I was thinking that myself, as a matter of fact," said Cody. He frowned.

Otis was frowning too. "Carl wouldn't steal a snowmobile and then go cruising around pretending to be looking for it."

Rae snapped her fingers. "I've got it. The snowmobile theft might have been a random prank by someone else. It's not necessarily related to everything else that's going on."

"She's right," Cody said. "Maybe we *should* concentrate on Carl. But we can't forget about the other suspects. Remember, each one has a motive."

When they got back to the lodge, they saw Mr. Warren standing at the front desk.

"Hi, kids," he said, and gave them a smile. "I'm just trying to check on the phone service." He tapped his fingers on the counter.

A clerk walked behind the desk. "Oh, Mr. Warren, it's you again. I'm sorry, but we have no phone service yet. I'm sure they will be sending snowplows soon."

Mrs. Crane walked over and put her hand on Mr. Warren's arm. "You checked on the phones again?

Don't worry, Frank. I'm not in such a hurry to get out of here as before. I think I overreacted to what happened. Joshua says he isn't the least bit worried."

Mr. Warren blinked a few times. Then he smiled again. "Great. We can spend some more time here as a family." He took her hand. "We'll be a family soon, won't we?"

"Of course we will," she said.

"I'm really looking forward to being a father to Joshua."

"Well, that's wonderful, Frank. Don't pressure him, though. Joshua has been pretty much on his own, you know. The way he's been competing and traveling, he's very grown up."

They started walking away together. "I'm looking forward to helping Joshua with his career," he said. "You know, I'll bet the right promotion could help him. I worked in advertising before I started my own business. I could help him get sponsors."

"Oh, there's no need," said Mrs. Crane, waving away his suggestion. "Coach Renner does that. After all, he has the motivation. His contract gives him a percentage of Joshua's prize money and sponsors' money."

Rae and the twins watched them walk away. Then they told Oscar about the wounded cougar. When he hurried away to dispatch the animal patrol, they talked about what they had just overheard.

"You heard what Mrs. Crane said." Otis rubbed his eyes. "We should have figured that the coaches would get a cut of the prize money. I thought they just got paid to coach. Whoever gets the most attention in Aspen will attract the most sponsors. The coaches have more at stake in having a winner than just their reputation."

"That's true," said Cody. "But let's follow through on our lead with Carl. He wasn't working the lift, so he must be around here somewhere."

Rae tilted her head to one side and grinned. "It's almost lunchtime. I bet I know where he is. Follow me to the dining room."

The dining room was empty. But when they walked into the kitchen, they saw Carl standing in front of the open refrigerator. He was holding Trent's vitamin drink in his hand. The three of them gasped.

Carl turned and looked at them. "What?" he asked. He put the bottle back in the refrigerator. "You think I'm terrible for coming in for a snack? So sue me. If you guys wanna rat me out and tell Oscar, I'll tell him where you were today. I'll bet he'll think it's worse than snagging a slice of cheese."

He shut the door and looked at them. He took a bite out of the slice of Swiss cheese he was holding. "So what's it gonna be?"

Rae swallowed. "We aren't going to tell about the cheese. B-but why were you holding Trent's vitamin drink?"

Carl squinted at her. "What are you talking about?" He blinked. "Oh, is that what's in that bottle? Don't worry; I wasn't going to drink it. It was in front of the Swiss cheese, that's all. You guys sure are nosy."

They all trooped out of the kitchen. Now it was Cody's turn to be brave. "Uh—Carl? What did you think of that avalanche?"

"I dunno. It was an avalanche. They happen all the time." He glanced at Cody as he kept walking. His long strides soon left Rae and the twins behind.

"Hang on, Carl," Cody called after him. "Did you see the avalanche? We were almost *in* it so we couldn't really see it. It must have looked *awesome.*"

Carl didn't even slow down. "I didn't see it, and I don't care. I've seen an avalanche before, more than once, too. It's no big deal. I was on my break, anyway."

Rae and the twins scurried after him. They had to think of a way to slow him down.

"Come on, Carl, wait up and talk to us," Rae piped up. "If you didn't watch the avalanche, what were you doing at the time?" She knew the question sounded suspicious.

Carl stopped and faced them. "What's with the questions? Are you guys writing a book or something?"

"Actually, we were just trying to get to know you better," said Otis. "We were wondering what you're interested in. Like—what did you do on your break that day?"

Carl rocked from side to side. "You're interested in me? Yeah, sure. That day on my break I watched TV in the game room, okay? Is that interesting? Now leave me alone." He turned to go.

"Wait a minute, Carl," Otis said firmly. "You did *not* watch TV in the game room. So what *did* you do that day?"

Carl whirled around. "What is wrong with you guys? I said I watched TV and that's what I did. End of story."

"No, Carl," said Otis. "You didn't watch TV in the game room, because that TV is broken."

Carl's eyes wavered. "No—no, it isn't."

A dull red flush began creeping up Carl's neck. Then it flooded into his face.

"We know you're lying, Carl," said Rae. "Where were you during the avalanche? You weren't in the game room."

[Chapter Thirteen]

Carl gritted his teeth. "It's none of your business where I was," he growled. "I don't have to tell you guys anything." He strode out the front door.

"It looks like Carl is our man," Cody said.

"He looked guilty all right, and he probably *is* guilty. But we can prove absolutely nothing. Zilch. Zero," said Rae.

"But he was in the kitchen before Trent was poisoned. He was near the bomb crater today. He wouldn't tell us where he was during the avalanche. *And* he has a grudge against Trent and Josh." Cody ran out of breath. His shoulders sagged. "I see what you mean. We don't have *proof*."

"Hello again, kids." Mr. Warren waved to them and gave them a big smile. "Going to lunch soon?"

"In a minute," Otis said, barely looking at him. He was trying to think of the missing link that would prove that Carl was guilty.

"Hi, guys," said Coach Renner breezily. Then he crossed paths with Mr. Warren.

Coach Renner held his hand up in a stop sign. "You can say hello, but don't say anything about my coaching, Frank," he said. "I don't mean to offend you, but that's the way it has to be."

Mr. Warren laughed. "I wasn't going to say anything about it. I've learned my lesson. I just wanted to say that Joshua was looking good."

He studied Mr. Warren's face. "I know I've said this before, and you say I'm wrong, but I feel like I've seen you somewhere."

Mr. Warren chuckled. "I've gotten that all my life. Almost every day somebody tells me they know me from somewhere. I guess I look like a lot of people. They're all lucky." He laughed at his own joke.

It's weird, thought Cody. *I'm starting to think I've seen him somewhere before, too. Is he somebody famous in disguise?* Cody didn't come up with anything.

Oscar came bustling over, tugging at his mustache. "I have wonderful news," he announced. He clasped his hands in front of his chest. "At last, the phones are working! Also, the snowplows have been clearing away the snow all morning. The road will be passable early this evening."

"Good news makes me hungry!" Cody exclaimed.

"Let's see, what should I have after lunch?" He closed his eyes. "Apple tart, cheesecake, fudge sundae . . . it's so hard to choose."

Otis rolled his eyes. "Haven't you had them all already? You've had dessert after lunch and dinner every day we've been here."

"I haven't had dessert *every day*."

"Have, too."

"I have *not*. At least not after lunch *and* dinner."

"Yes. You. Have." Otis looked him in the eye. "Besides, you should be thinking of how to solve this case, not dessert."

They went over the clues again. "We've decided that Carl is probably the one who has been causing all the so-called 'accidents,'" said Rae quietly to the group. "We just have to find the last piece of the puzzle that will hang the guilty sign around his neck."

"Better hurry. We're going to pack up and leave tomorrow morning," said Mr. Carson.

"I'm still not convinced that someone is up to something deliberate," said Maxim as he buttered a piece of bread.

"And avalanches happen naturally all the time," Mr. Carson added.

"But—" Cody began. He stopped suddenly when Otis gave him a warning look. He drew in his breath sharply. He had been about to tell Maxim and his father about the bomb crater. That wouldn't have been a good move.

Otis's brain was working furiously, though he was sitting perfectly still. He gazed around the dining room. Coach Renner was sitting at a table with Joshua. The two were deep in conversation. Coach Kent sat at a table with Trent. Mrs. Crane was sitting by herself, fiddling with her engagement ring again.

"Better start eating, Otis. Your hamburger is getting cold," Rae whispered, giving him a little nudge. Cody was already digging into his hot fudge sundae.

Otis wrenched his attention away from where it was wandering.

He bit into his hamburger. No matter how worried he was about the case, the burger was still good. He wolfed it down.

Otis sighed. There wasn't much time left to solve this case. He chewed his last french fry. "Do you think we could stay a little longer, Dad?"

Mr. Carson dropped his fork. "Oh, Otis, I think this trip has come to an end."

"Trent and Joshua are leaving anyway," said Maxim. "Maybe we'll go see them in Aspen at the Silver Creek Challenge."

"Yeah, I'd like to see them at the games," Otis said.

The waiter brought the check. "I'll get this," said Maxim. He handed the waiter a credit card. When the waiter returned with his card, Maxim studied the bill. "All right, what's twenty percent of eighty-eight fifty?"

"Seventeen seventy," Rae and the twins said together.

"Very good." Maxim smiled. "That's the tip." He scribbled the amount on the bill and signed his name. "All done. We can go now."

Otis was trying so hard to put things together, his head was starting to hurt. There was a clue knocking on the door to his brain, whispering, *Open up and let me in.*

After lunch, he decided to go for a walk by himself. He stuck his hands in his pockets and shuffled along. As he walked, he looked down at the rug, as if hoping to find the answer written there. He heard voices as people passed him.

"I want *you* to coach him. He can do that trick. Trent can be the best there is. I know he can. He's got the skill; he just needs help with the technique. He needs someone to give him confidence, not hold him back. I'm not satisfied with Kent, and even *you* know that Trent is better than Joshua."

"I don't know about that. Trent and Joshua are different. I'll think about coaching Trent, but I won't have him try the trick you're talking about yet. It's too dangerous, Maggie. It's an inverted trick. He'll be hanging upside down in midair. He's too young."

"He can do it!"

It was Maggie arguing with Coach Renner. She was pushing him. She didn't seem to care how dangerous the trick was.

Otis remembered that Maggie would get lots of money if something happened to Trent. A chill ran through him.

As they passed each other, Maggie stopped talking for a moment. "Hi, Otis," she said, and gave him a big smile.

Otis smiled back. *Would she really hurt Trent?*

Suddenly he had an idea that had nothing to do with Maggie. It wasn't all there yet, but it was a start.

[Chapter Fourteen]

Otis headed back to the dining room. He found Oscar going over the dinner menu.

"Hi, Oscar."

The man looked up from his work and smiled. "Hello, Otis. Did you enjoy your lunch?"

"It was great," Otis said. "Especially the dessert. In fact, dessert is what I want to talk to you about. See, Cody and I have something to settle. I think he had dessert after lunch and dinner every single day we've been here. He says he hasn't, but I know he's wrong."

Oscar chuckled. "I'm on your side. Cody is definitely a fan of our desserts here."

"I know I'm right," said Otis, "but I have to prove it. Could I see the dining room receipts beginning with Monday? I can find out how many desserts are on our checks. Would you mind? Is it too much trouble?"

Oscar twisted his mustache and grinned. "Happy

to help," he said as he jumped up. "I'll get the receipts from the office."

He hurried away and came back with stacks of receipts in rubber bands. "You can take the ones that are yours and show them to Cody. You'll have to bring them back, though."

"Thanks." Otis took the bundles to a table and went through them. It didn't take long to find the one he was looking for. It was Frank Warren's from dinner on Monday, the day Trent got sick.

He remembered that Frank said he'd forgotten to leave a tip for the waiter. But he paid with a credit card. He'd seen Frank take the card from the waiter's hand.

Usually when people pay with a credit card they write the tip on the bill. That is what Maxim had just done after lunch. Otis held Frank Warren's bill from Monday in his hand. Frank had left a tip on the check. So why had he returned to the dining room to leave a tip in cash?

Otis's mind whirled. *Maybe*, he thought, *it was because Mr. Warren realized that someone might smell the ipecac in the bottle. Trent couldn't smell it in his drink because he had a bad cold, but someone else might have. Mr. Warren could have gone back to the dining room to pick up the bottle, which would explain why it had been rinsed clean.*

Otis put the bill in his pocket. It meant something, he was *sure* of it. It was the clue that had been nagging him for so long. But the more he walked, the more doubtful he became about his new theory.

Mr. Warren was a nice guy. He was saner than anybody in the group surrounding Josh and Trent. Otis took the bill out of his pocket and looked at it again. The guy probably just forgot about writing the tip down, that's all. *So much for my big breakthrough.*

Mr. Warren walked past him. "Hi, Otis," he said. He flashed his usual smile and gave him a cheery wave. Otis ducked his head as he waved back. He was ashamed of himself for suspecting such a nice guy.

I'll have to go back and tell Rae and Cody that I haven't figured anything out, he thought miserably. He passed through the lobby on his way to the game room.

"Hey, Otis!" Joshua called to him.

"Hi, Josh."

"Are you guys leaving, or are you sticking around?"

"My dad wants to leave soon," Otis said. He glanced around the lobby. Maggie was standing at the desk with her back to them. The yellow pages were open on the counter, and she was talking on the phone. Mrs. Crane was standing nearby, looking nervous and worried.

"Maybe you can talk him into staying longer,"

Joshua said. "Coach decided we didn't have to leave, so we'll be here another week." He glanced at his mother. "Mr. Warren is staying, too. I think he and my mom will get married soon."

"Um—that's great." Otis wasn't sure Joshua would agree.

"Yeah, I guess so," he said. "Mr. Warren is okay. I wish he'd stop trying to be so buddy-buddy with me, but I do want my mom to be happy."

Over at the desk, Otis saw Maggie hang up the phone and walk away. The phone rang again a moment later, and the clerk called to Mrs. Crane. She raced over to take the call as though she'd been waiting for it for hours. She kept shaking her head. Otis thought it must be bad news. For a woman who was getting married, she didn't look very happy at all.

Otis looked back at Joshua and noticed a long smudgy streak on the sleeve of his jacket. "Hey, Josh, look at that," he pointed.

Joshua glanced at his sleeve and saw the smudge. "How'd *that* get there?" He sniffed a few times. "It smells weird, too."

Out of the corner of his eye, Otis saw Mrs. Crane slam the phone into its cradle. Then she rushed away with that bustling, choppy stride of hers and ran up the stairs. Her fists were clenched at her sides. Joshua followed her, looking concerned. "See you around, Otis."

Otis caught a strange smell as Joshua walked by. What was it? The smell was familiar, but he couldn't identify it.

There was a pad lying on the desk. Otis decided to take some paper with him to make notes about what had been happening. He tore off the top sheet of paper and headed for the game room.

Otis smoothed out the piece of paper he'd torn from the pad at the desk. "Let's make a list of suspects and clues," he said. "Who has a pen?"

Rae handed him a pencil.

"Thanks." Otis looked down at the paper. "Somebody wrote something on the pad," he said, "and it's left an impression on this page," he said.

He carefully shaded over what was written using the side of the pencil lead. When he finished, the letters and numbers stood out in white against the gray background.

"It looks like a phone number and a reference number," Otis said. "Let's give the number a call."

"We can use the phone right here," said Rae.

"Let me do it," Cody said, reaching for the piece of paper.

"Sure." Otis handed it to him. "I saw Maggie and Mrs. Crane both use the phone at the desk. Maybe one of them jotted down some information."

"We'll find out." Cody dialed the number. He nodded when someone answered. "I'm calling about number TR770889W," he said, and waited. His eyes widened. He picked up the pencil and began writing on the piece of paper. "No, there is no change. I'm his assistant. Can you tell me when the reservation was made? Ah, this morning at eleven o'clock. Thank you."

Cody hung up. "Wait till you hear this," he said. "Frank Warren made a plane reservation. A coach seat to Los Angeles tonight at nine o'clock. *For one person.*"

"But Joshua said that they were staying on another week," Otis said. "I assumed that Mr. Warren was staying, too." He tapped his fingers on the table. "He didn't say for sure. But he *did* say that his mother and Mr. Warren would probably get married soon. Mrs. Crane didn't look too happy when I saw her today, though."

"Who knows why?" Rae said. "There could be a million reasons."

Otis pulled the lunch bill from his pocket. "Here's something else," he said. "Mr. Warren's receipt from lunch the other day. I kept thinking there was something wrong, because when people pay with a credit card they usually put the tip on the check. Mr. Warren *did* add a tip, but then he said he didn't."

Rae and Cody looked at the check. "That's really weird," said Cody.

"It sure is," Rae said. She glanced at her watch. "Does it lead somewhere or not? How can we find out?" She pursed her lips. "I've got an idea. Maybe the maids know something. Maxim said maids know everything about guests."

As it turned out, the maids were easy to find. One of them was standing outside Frank Warren's room. She and Mr. Warren were having an argument. The other maid was standing behind a laundry cart, watching.

"That's Jane behind the laundry cart," said Rae. "Shelly is the one arguing with Mr. Warren. I met them when we first got to the resort."

Shelly waved her arms around angrily. "Don't you talk to me that way," she said. "I'm *not* stupid. The DO NOT DISTURB sign was on the hallway floor, not on the doorknob. I knocked and you didn't answer. *Twice.* So I thought it was okay to go in and clean the room."

"You aren't supposed to *think*," Mr. Warren shouted. "You're supposed to do what the sign says. *Do not disturb.*"

The twins and Rae looked at each other. "Can that really be Mr. Warren?" Rae whispered. "He's being really nasty."

"You weren't inside!" Shelly shouted back. "So I wasn't disturbing you."

"I ought to report you to the management, but I don't have time." Mr. Warren slammed the door.

Jane pulled Shelly away. "Let's go. You shouldn't have been yelling at a guest."

"All right, all right." They walked down the hall. Rae and the twins caught up with them.

"Hi, Shelly. Hi, Jane." Rae waved hello. "Um . . . was that Mr. Warren who was shouting?"

Shelly turned to look at Rae. Her expression was so sour that Otis thought she might tell Rae to mind her own business. But she didn't. "He must have gotten up on the wrong side of the bed," she grumbled.

"Something must be wrong," Jane said as she wheeled the cart around a corner. "That nice Mr. Warren never acted that way before, did he?"

"No." Shelly shook her head. "I saw a suitcase open on Mr. Warren's bed, and there were these strange goggles in there." She patted her hair. "I picked them up because they looked like some I saw on TV. My son and I were watching a show the other night, and this guy had on night-vision goggles. My son thought they were really cool. I figured he'd like it if I told him one of the guests had some."

Rae was nodding and smiling. "Night-vision glasses *are* cool. What did they look like?"

"They had this headpiece, sort of like a helmet with cutaway pieces. Hard to describe. Anyway, I was holding them up and looking at them when Mr. Warren walked in."

Rae stopped smiling but she kept nodding. "So he was angry, right?"

Shelly rolled her eyes. "I'll say. He grabbed the goggles out of my hand and started yelling about the DO NOT DISTURB sign. No matter what I said, he just kept getting more and more steamed."

Jane tapped her on the shoulder. "Forget about him. He'll be gone soon anyway. I saw him checking out. We have to finish these rooms if *we're* ever going to get out of here today."

"Okay," Shelly said. "Gotta go now. So long." Shelly waved good-bye to Rae and the twins, took some clean towels from the cart, and followed Jane into a room.

"Nice work, Rae," said Otis.

"Thanks."

Everything started falling into place, fitting together like the pieces of a puzzle. "Mr. Warren could easily have been the one to poison Trent's vitamin drink," Cody said.

"He's definitely strong enough to have placed those rocks on the jump course," said Rae.

"There is something else," Otis said quickly. "Joshua had a smudge on his jacket, and it smelled strange. It smelled just like that goop in the bomb crater. The first day we were here, we overheard Joshua complaining that Mr. Warren was always borrowing his stuff. It was Mr. Warren who set off the dynamite wearing Joshua's jacket, and he was probably the one who fired the gun that day we saw the cougar."

"But wait—one thing I don't get. It was *Joshua* who was attacked and stranded on the ski lift, not Trent. Why would Mr. Warren want to hurt the athlete whose money he wanted?" Cody asked.

"I can answer that," said Rae. "I overheard Carl saying that Josh's missing clothes were found tied to the chairlift. Carl was saying how weird it was that the jacket was *Trent's*, not Josh's. Josh must have put on the wrong one when he went outside that night."

"Plus, he probably had his hat and ski mask on to keep warm. Mr. Warren wouldn't have been able to recognize Josh—even with the help of night-vision goggles," said Otis.

"It would have been easy to mistake Joshua for Trent," added Rae. "They're about the same size."

Cody looked back toward Mr. Warren's room. "What are we going to do? He'll be leaving soon."

A sliver of light fell across the carpet in front of Mr. Warren's door, then it vanished. Rae and the twins ducked around the corner just in time. Mr. Warren stepped into the hallway. He was carrying a suitcase. He looked around cautiously. Then he headed in the direction of the parking lot.

[Chapter Fifteen]

"He's getting away!" Rae hissed.

Otis was supercharged. He turned to his brother. "I have an idea. Cody, run into the game room, call the desk, and ask for Mr. Warren. Pretend to be a sponsor with a lot of money to offer. Make up a name that sounds good. Rae, you hang around the desk. When the phone rings, the desk clerk will answer and he'll probably repeat Mr. Warren's name. Then you can offer to run outside and catch Mr. Warren so he won't miss his important phone call."

"I'll just talk like this," Cody said in a low bass. He could have been forty years old. Cody was a genius at disguising his voice. He could throw it, too.

"Good. Stall him as long as you can. Keep him on the phone. I want to fix his vehicle so that he can't go anywhere. It's that white van. I'll search it and see what

I can find. Give me as much time as you possibly can. Okay, everybody, let's go, go, go!"

Cody ran to the game room. Otis hurried toward the parking lot. Rae stood fidgeting by the desk. They all kept their fingers crossed, hoping Mr. Warren wouldn't get away.

The phone at the desk rang, and the desk clerk came out from the back and answered. "Mr. Warren? One moment, please. I'll see if he's still here."

Before he could ring Mr. Warren's room, Rae said, "I just saw him walk out. I'll go catch him." She didn't give the clerk a chance to answer. Instead, she sprinted for the parking lot, where Otis was waiting.

Rae got to the parking lot just as Mr. Warren was loading his suitcase into the back of his van. "Mr. Warren! Mr. Warren, wait! The clerk at the front desk sent me out to tell you that you've got a phone call."

Mr. Warren's eyes wavered. He was all ready to go, and his mind was already miles down the road.

"Hurry, Mr. Warren," Rae urged. "The clerk said it was a really, really important call."

"Who is it?"

"I don't know. He just said something about a sponsor and told me it was really important that you didn't miss the call."

Mr. Warren shut the back doors of the van. He hesitated a moment. "I'll take the call," he said.

As soon as Otis saw Mr. Warren walk away, he hurried to the van and opened the hood. He found the fuel line and cut it with his pocketknife. Then he rushed to the back of the vehicle.

He pulled open the doors of the van and climbed in. He tried to open the suitcase. At first he thought it was locked, but the hinges were just sticky. He flipped up the lid, and there were the night-vision goggles, right on top.

He took some deep breaths and tried to calm his racing heart. How much time did he have? He tried to send Cody a mental message to keep stalling. He could feel the sweat beading on his forehead.

Otis began rifling through the contents of the suitcase. He lifted shirts and pants and socks and even rolled-up underwear. Underneath the clothes were a few books. In a pouch on the lid there were belts and a pair of shoes. That was all.

Working frantically, Otis checked again. He found nothing but clothes and shoes and books.

A lump rose in his throat. How could there be nothing—not a shred of evidence in the suitcase? He'd been so *sure*.

He felt like he was suffocating. Now the van had a cut fuel line. And he had nothing to show for it. What if he'd been wrong? He looked through the window to see if anyone was coming.

His hands were shaking as he checked the clothes once more. He peered into the pouch inside the top of the case. Still, he found nothing.

Something has to be here, he told himself. His eyes searched the back of the van. Except for the suitcase, it was empty.

How long could Cody stall Mr. Warren? The man would start getting suspicious if Cody kept up his routine too long. He might be here any minute, and then Otis knew he'd be in serious trouble.

He bit his knuckles. He had to find something *right now*.

Otis began closing the suitcase again. Then, as he looked at it, a thought struck him. The suitcase seemed pretty deep, but it wasn't holding much.

He picked up the suitcase and shook it. It was significantly heavier than he had suspected it would be. It rattled. What was rattling in there? Otis opened the suitcase again. He glanced through the window. No one was coming . . . yet. As he removed the clothes and the books, he could hear his own heavy breathing.

He looked more carefully at the titles of the books: *The Winner's Life, Be a Doer Not a Loser, A Million Ways to Win, Loser No More.*

Wow, thought Otis, *this guy is obsessed with winning.*

He started carefully removing everything again. When the clothes and books were all lying beside the suitcase, he thumped his fist against the bottom of the case. There was a hollow sound. Otis knew then that the suitcase must have a false bottom. He pushed down on one of the corners, and part of the panel popped up. Otis pulled out the panel and gasped.

Frank Warren had a deadly drugstore hidden away in his suitcase. He had arsenic and sleeping pills, chloroform and snake venom, strychnine and cyanide. He had caffeine, which Otis knew could be deadly if the dose was large enough, and he had ipecac—enough to take out a whole Olympic *team,* not just one teenager. He had at least a dozen other bottles, all neatly labeled with long, tongue-twisting names. Otis didn't know what they were, but he was sure they were all harmful.

There was something else in the bottom of the suitcase. A shiny black handgun. Otis's heart skipped a beat, and he instinctively pulled his hands away. *No wonder the suitcase is so heavy,* he thought. *This guy is dangerous, all right. He could even be a murderer.*

Suddenly the back doors of the van swung open forcefully.

"Looking for something, Otis?"

Otis felt fear close around his heart. He turned slowly and came face-to-face with a Frank Warren he had never met. This man with his cold, expressionless eyes was a different human being from the cheery, friendly guy Otis knew. In fact, this man was like something inhuman, an evil robot.

"What am I going to do with you, Otis? You and the other two had to go snooping around. It was I who saved you from the cougar that day up by the bomb hole. I didn't like finding you guys up there, but I would have let it go." He shook his head in mock regret. "It looks like I'll have to take you someplace and make you disappear."

"I-I was just . . ." Otis stammered before he yanked open the van's sliding door, jumped out, and ran. He didn't get very far. Frank Warren was fast, and he was strong. He grabbed Otis from behind.

Otis called on all of the karate training that had made him a black belt. He found a way to calm his mind and focus, as his sensei had taught him. His body became his own secret weapon. In his hand he held the element of surprise.

He grabbed Mr. Warren's left wrist with his left hand and twisted. At the same time, he curved his toes up inside his boots and stomped on Warren's instep with his heel.

"*Argh!*" Mr. Warren groaned and staggered backward. He blinked and shook his head, trying to understand what had just happened.

Otis whirled around. Frank Warren's anger was stoked by pain now. He grabbed Otis by both shoulders and began to shake him. "You little troublemaker!" he snarled through clenched teeth.

Otis shot both arms up and out, breaking the angry man's hold. Mr. Warren bent down and lunged at him. Otis stomped his instep again and shoved Mr. Warren's chin back hard with the heel of his hand.

Frank Warren howled in pain and fury. He was beginning to get the idea that Otis wasn't going to be pushed around as easily as he had thought.

Cody and Rae came running into the parking lot and raced toward Mr. Warren. Cody went into a Spread Eagle Stance. Frank Warren's eyes flickered between Cody and Otis, unsure what to make of the twins and their surprising skills. In a superfast, smooth move, Cody leaned back a little with his weight on his left foot. He bent his right foot up and back, then smashed the ball of his foot into Mr. Warren's shin. *Whack!*

Frank Warren bellowed with rage. He brought his arm back and struck out, trying to backhand Cody across the face. Cody dodged the blow and stepped back to ready for a counterattack. But in a stroke of bad luck, his toe caught in a pothole and knocked him off balance. He fell backward and landed on his backside. *Thud!* He gasped as the painful landing knocked the wind out of him.

Rae faced Mr. Warren defiantly. He lunged for her, and she side-stepped. He fell forward, landing on his hands and knees. But he was up again in an instant.

Otis whirled and hit him with a backward heel stomp. "Go get help, Rae!" he gasped. "We've got this, but get help!"

As Mr. Warren lunged for his throat, Otis grabbed his wrist and twisted. Holding his wrist, Otis turned his back and hooked his foot behind Mr. Warren's leg. He wrenched it forward in a leg sweep.

Rae was sprinting toward the lodge. Mr. Warren glanced at her and in a split second he weighed his options. Fighting this kid wasn't easy. He was hurting now, and others would arrive soon. It would be better to get away.

Instead of lunging for Otis, Mr. Warren yanked the door of the van open and leaped into the driver's seat. He locked the doors and shoved the key into the ignition. He turned the key, but nothing happened. He turned it again. Still nothing. Through the window he saw Otis shaking his head.

Mr. Warren realized that the car had been tampered with. His face turned a purplish red, and he pounded on the steering wheel. In a flash, he unlocked the door and jumped out of the van.

"Right behind you!" Cody called to him. But Cody *wasn't* behind him. He was hiding behind a car, using a trick he'd been perfecting for a long time. He was throwing his voice.

Frank Warren whirled around and found himself face-to-face with . . . nobody. Then Cody threw his voice again. "Now I'm over here!"

Mr. Warren took the bait again and again, turning around and around in confusion. He gnashed his teeth. Finally, he paid no attention to the voice. He lunged at Otis.

Otis was ready and waiting. The instant Frank Warren bent over to grab him, he cupped both hands and swung them straight at his ears—*thwack!*

The ear slap sent Mr. Warren staggering backward,

roaring and holding his head. With his eyes squeezed shut, he collapsed onto the ground.

Suddenly, a black sedan sped into the parking lot. It screeched to a halt in front of Otis and Mr. Warren. A big, beefy man jumped out and strode over. He looked down at Frank Warren. "It looks like you met your match, pal," he said.

Then he turned to Otis. "I'm Roger Madison, Private Investigator." He opened his wallet and showed his card. "I was hired by Mrs. Crane to shadow this character and dig into his past. What I found was very *bad* news, any way you slice it. I called the police, and they'll be here soon."

He gave Otis a pat on the back. "I saw some of your moves when I was driving up. You did some job. You could fight on my team any day."

Cody was pushing himself to his feet. "*Whew!* I feel like the heavy bag after a workout at Gold's Boxing Gym. I had to fight with my voice."

"I'm glad you did, too. Thanks." Otis looked at Roger Madison. "Our sensei teaches that it's always better to get away than to fight. But Mr. Warren was totally freaking me out. He came at me and said he was going to take me somewhere."

"You did what you had to do," said the investigator.

Four police cruisers pulled up. The officers got out. One of them helped Frank Warren to his feet and slapped him in handcuffs. Mr. Warren listened sullenly as the officer read him his rights.

"You have the right to remain silent . . ."

Frank Warren fixed a hateful gaze on Cody, Otis, and Rae. "I got so close to winning this time! If you kids hadn't gotten in my way, I would have managed an Olympic medalist *and* his money!"

Everyone poured out of the lodge. Mrs. Crane stood by, twisting her ring around and around her finger.

Just before Mr. Warren was put in the police cruiser, Mrs. Crane walked over to him. She took off her ring and stuffed it in the pocket of his jacket. "It's a fake anyway," she said. "Just like you."

[Chapter Sixteen]

After the police officer pulled away with Frank Warren in the car, other officers questioned the guests. It took a few hours. By the time the police cruisers pulled out of the parking lot, everyone was both edgy and relieved, and exhausted, too. Oscar gathered them in the lobby and brought in coffee, tea, milk, and cookies. Roger Madison, the private investigator, got up and explained why he'd been investigating Frank Warren.

"This guy is bad news," he said. "He asked Mrs. Crane to marry him, but she got a little suspicious. That was smart, Mrs. Crane."

"He was vague about what he did for a living," she explained. "He seemed obsessed with having the perfect family. At times I thought he was putting on an act, pretending to be somebody else. Then he gave me the fake diamond ring. I didn't care about having a real diamond—but a lie is never good." She clasped her hands in front of her. "I had to be careful about the man who could be Joshua's stepfather."

"You were right to do that, Mrs. Crane. I found other women he'd tried to scam. He always picked a single mother with a boy who was an athlete." He tapped his forehead with his index finger. "You see, this guy is a sicko. He's a frustrated athlete himself who wants to live the life he never had through the boys. He wants to get in on the money they'll make, too."

Coach Renner snapped his fingers. "I *knew* I recognized him from somewhere. It was years ago, at the Branford Games. I was a young coach, just starting out, not much older than the athletes I was coaching. A friend of mine was coaching for the club Frank Warren belonged to. He pointed him out to me—he was about seventeen then. My friend said that Frank had some talent, but he never wanted to put the time into training. Then he started playing dirty tricks on his teammates and opponents, so my friend dropped him."

"Now I remember where I saw him, too!" Otis said. "Dad took Cody and me to the Deerville Winter Sports Games. This guy kept hanging around one of the contestants. She kept telling him to get lost, waving him away. Finally, he made a scene and the officials told him to stay away."

"That sounds like him. He'd try to take over all the coaching and all the managing. When things didn't work out for him, he got angry. He never killed anyone, but a couple of times people got pretty sick. Poisoning is his specialty. He's used ipecac before."

"I can't even hear that *word* without feeling sick," said Trent.

Madison continued, "He got away with money and jewelry, too. You'd better check to make sure you're not missing anything, Mrs. Crane."

"I already checked," said Mrs. Crane. "Nothing's missing."

"I think that's because these three, Otis, Cody, and Rae, figured he was up to something and made him uncomfortable," said Madison. "He seemed to be in a big hurry to get out of here."

"I think he knew we were onto him," Otis agreed. "At least he was getting worried."

"It's a good thing, too," said Joshua. "He would have hurt somebody else. It sounds like he was getting more and more desperate. He wouldn't have had all those poisons if he hadn't considered using them."

"I've heard about ipecac," said Trent, making a face as he said the word. "It can do a lot more than make you sick. It can kill you." He stood up and leaned against the wall. "Mr. Warren had to be a monster to take a chance like that." Trent looked down for a moment. When he looked up, he was smiling. "You guys saved my life TWICE!"

"Thanks for saving us both," said Joshua. He shook hands with Rae and the twins.

"One thing still bothers me," said Cody. "Carl, where were you really during the avalanche? You couldn't have been watching TV because the satellite was out."

"Okay, okay, I'll tell you about it," Carl said, hunching over in his chair. "On my break, I prac-tice snowboarding in the terrain park or the half-pipe when Joshua and Trent are somewhere else."

"Why'd you keep it a secret?" Trent asked.

Carl gave a clumsy shrug. "You guys weren't exactly friendly," he said. "I didn't think it would be okay."

"Things are different now," said Joshua. "It's all right with us. We'll even show you some tricks, right, Trent?"

"Yeah, why not?" Trent agreed.

Joshua turned to Rae and the twins. "So, can you all stick around and go snowboarding with us?"

Otis, Cody, and Rae looked at Mr. Carson. He nodded to them. "We may as well stay," he said, "now that there's no crazed psychopath running around. I'm so glad that everyone is all right."

*

After another few days of snowboarding, Otis, Cody, and Rae returned home to Deerville. The Carsons' family hound, Dude, and their parrot, Pauly, were happy to see them. It was good to be home.

A few weeks later, they were all sitting in the den when Maxim said, "Look at this: Joshua and Trent both got their pictures in the newspaper." He peered over the pages. "It's good news. They both did very well at the Silver Creek Challenge and tied in total number of points. The paper calls them 'young Olympic hopefuls to watch.'"

Otis, Cody, and Rae all grinned. "Don't forget, they promised us a seat to any event they were competing in," said Otis.

"So I guess that means . . ." Rae nodded to Cody.

". . . we're going to the Olympics!" Cody finished, pumping a fist in the air.

This got Pauly very excited. He danced from one side of his perch to the other, screeching, "Pauly to the Olympics! Pauly to the Olympics! Pauly to the Olympics!"

"Shh, Pauly!" Rae held a finger to her lips. "You'll

wake up Dude." She stroked the head of the sleeping dog. Dude rolled onto his side and started to snore.

"I'm going to the kitchen to get a soda," said Otis. He stepped over Dude.

"*Step on no pets*," said Cody, seizing an opportunity for a palindrome.

"*Doggone it*, Cody, give the palindromes a rest," retorted Otis. He chuckled at his own pun.

Rae sighed. "Will you guys ever stop with that stuff?"

"No," said Cody and Otis together. A mischievous smile appeared on Cody's lips.

"Uh-oh," said Rae. "Did you just come up with *another* palindrome?"

Cody nodded. "We said our *nos in unison*."

Rae rolled her eyes, then grinned at her cousins. They were so weird sometimes, but she had to admit that life without them would be pretty dull.